Ravenous

An Enemies to Lovers BWWM Contemporary Romance

By Cali Burem

Contents

Prologue: First Taste

Six months ago

-

"Well, *Merry Christmas*," Mia said, appreciatively.

"First off, this is March. Second, did you just objectify that man before I had a chance to?" Mia's friend Max didn't have the decency to resist moaning around the straw in his mouth when he saw the ass his friend was ogling.

The man definitely did squats.

Dressed in beautifully tailored black slacks, a crisp gray shirt and a black silk tie, the man who'd just entered the room was turning heads and causing all sorts of conversation to halt.

"Shall we move closer so we can breathe deeply from his well of pheromones?" Max asked.

Mia didn't respond.

The man had just turned and raised his face and she grimaced openly as her brain supplied some vital information.

She *knew* him.

She'd know that man anywhere.

'That man' just happened to be Westley Nott, someone she was sure had been born to be the good-looking version of the back end of a horse.

It had been almost four years since she'd seen him last- during the first chance she'd been given representing a small organization and she'd lost, all because of him.

His dark hair gleamed under the soft lighting of the banquet hall and when he gave someone a warm smile, Mia frowned.

She remembered his face and body, aware of it and his ability to still draw the attention of everyone in a room.

Time had only served to make him even more gorgeous and Mia felt an unfair anger directed at the universe.

She'd seen him on TV and in magazines and newspapers, eligible bachelor that he was, but today was the first time she'd seen him in person again in all that time and she didn't know what she would do if she actually met him face-to-face.

2

She doubted he even remembered her anyway.

Assholes rarely thought of those affected by their behaviour.

Westley Nott had been the reason she'd lost a case with her first major corporate client after a series of wins with smaller ones.

Mia had worked her butt off after that and to hear her CEO tell it, she had never gotten over it, even years after the fact, even being a successful lawyer and generally happy with her life and results… even then, just seeing him standing there made her want to escape before he made her feel less than significant. Like he was about to undermine every aspect of her career with a glance and a flippant word once again.

"I can't believe he's here," she said to Max as she continued to watch Westley while searching for an exit.

Max didn't notice her unease, still openly ogling the man. Their friend Leah introduced Westley to a woman in a gown who smiled invitingly at him. Leah was small and pretty with her hair braided into tiny twists, brown eyes and brown skin, a shade lighter than Mia's.

Max licked his lips. "He is disgustingly straight but I would definitely watch the two of you have sex."

Mia snorted at that, light brown eyes bright with amusement for a second. "The highest of praise coming from you but I wouldn't be caught dead anywhere near him."

"Why not? You're single, go get him," Max said, nudging her. His green eyes were filled with barely contained mischief and Mia tried to keep her face neutral.

She mumbled, "I'm not," and received the expected eye roll.

Max gave her a no-nonsense look and she didn't even need him to speak to know he was not interested in even mentioning her ex who had left their apartment and a note on her fridge saying he needed to find himself.

She didn't need Max telling her off for that. That was Leah's job.

Small, sweet Leah was *sick* of Eric and that was part of the reason she'd invited Mia out for a night spent mingling with hot eligible bachelors who weren't wishy-washy about commitments- at least not monetary commitments.

Max and Leah were Mia's closest friends, had been since their first year of university together, and the party being thrown was a celebration of the success of Leah's first major event, the Lusaka Artist Festival. After months of Leah meticulously planning and freaking out, it had been a major success and she was already getting calls to handle other events.

From what Mia could tell by just watching them Leah and Westley were apparently on friendly terms but she wondered why Leah had never mentioned him to her. Or warned her.

She supposed she *had* mentioned him to them but she hadn't mentioned him after that day. One day of whining and cursing him and buying a voodoo doll online had been enough and she'd unhealthily suppressed her feelings of hatred for the man.

She had told Max and Leah that she'd lost and they'd comforted her but she hadn't spoken of him again after, content to stew until time healed her. But time must have dropped out of med school because it was four years later and seeing him made her feel like they were in that boardroom again and he was laughing at her presentation.

Westley had made her doubt herself and her doubt had stayed with her, driving her to prove him wrong. Someone who had never even given her a second thought after.

There was no reason for her to feel so off-kilter.

He was a different person, older now. And besides, if he was still an ass, she was older and several self-defense classes wiser now. One wrong word from him and she could put him in the hospital.

She sighed and heard a soft tearing sound.

She quickly looked down at the black dress she was in and cursed loudly. An old man gave her a saucy grin for her language and she laughed awkwardly before she turned back to face her problem.

The dress was one of Leah's.

Mia had completely forgotten to carry her own with her to get changed at Leah's for the event. It was too far from her place to go back home in the evening traffic. Leah had come through with the number and they'd managed to get her into it.

Leah's dress was a little tight for her and seemed to overly accentuate every curve of her body. The chest area in particular, while being low cut and elegant on the smaller Leah, almost came off as totally indecent on her. She felt like she had to breathe slowly and carefully just so it wouldn't burst at the seams.

"He's coming this way!"

Mia looked up abruptly with a gasp and then both she and Max turned to look down at her dress at the loud ripping sound. Her sudden movement had caused the already low cut design of the dress to somehow split evenly down her cleavage, now being held together by three overworking strands of cotton and a prayer.

Mia looked up in panic and Max stood in front of her hurriedly, blocking the view of her almost overflowing breasts to anyone else in the room.

He turned to the curtain beside them and sighed with relief. "A balcony, come on."

He led her outside into the warm night air and together they tried to see what could be done about the dress.

"We either need a professional seamstress or a coat and a ride home. I'll go look for both," he said, brushing his curls out of his eyes, something Mia found endearing but that she knew he did to add to his boyish charm. "In the meantime, drink this."

He handed her his glass of wine and she took it. She smiled gratefully as he took off, leaving her there in the shadows, leaning against the iron railing.

She waited, looking out at the night sky and fretting with the dress only to have one of the faithful strands give up. She left it then and decided to wait.

Ten minutes later, the curtains were pulled back.

Mia stepped away from the railing and out of the shadows, looking down at her dress and trying not to fiddle with it too much, "*Finally*. I thought you'd forgotten all about me."

"Ugh, another one?"

Mia looked up and met beautiful blue eyes.

Westley Nott.

She blinked at him, lifting her hands to hide the obscene amount of unintentional cleavage she was presently thrusting into his line of vision.

But good heavens, he was *a god*.

A good head taller than her, broad-shouldered and *absolutely* gorgeous...

She wondered absently if he'd give her the same sexy grin he'd been throwing around in the hall but his mouth thinned as he took in her state, an expression she found oddly familiar. His gaze lingered for a moment on her long dark hair - the untamed coils and curls falling over one side, framing her heart-shaped face. The dress, tight but flowing out once it reached her hips hid her long legs underneath.

"I'm sorry but I'm not interested," the man said curtly after a moment.

Mia looked up at him in confusion after a second. "I'm sorry?"

"I said I'm not interested."

When Mia continued to look like a confused duckling, head tilted to the side, he sighed.

"Look, you're a beautiful woman. You could do so much better than this and-"

It dawned on her and her eyes narrowed. "You think I'm some sort of… common tart?"

"I'm sure you're one of the more," his gaze went the length of her body appreciatively. "*Elite* escorts-"

She reacted before she could think and threw her drink at him. Considering she'd already drank most of it, it was mostly a couple of drops that splashed his shirt.

Westley looked down at his shirt and then up at her with the hint of a smile on his lips.

The man had the *balls* to be amused at that.

"Still an arrogant, unbelievable, *ill-mannered-*" she spoke angrily as she walked toward him. She was going to murder him, she was sure of it. Throw him off the balcony; make it look like an accident-

"Hey honey, got some pins and-"

Max stopped in his tracks, looking from her to Wes and then back to her.

"Um…"

Mia seemed to remember herself and abruptly walked away as it dawned on Westley that she was actually one of the guests there and hadn't snuck in to try to seduce him.

She stormed passed a couple of people who stared at her chest unabashedly. She had been going to the door, determined to drive around the city to cool down, when she saw it there, being placed on the table like an invite from a mischievous demon.

***

"Wow, you really fucked up."

Wes was running a hand through his hair irritably. "How was I to know she wasn't a-"

"Strumpet? Whore? Lady of the quarter to midnight?"

He groaned and Max chuckled. "It was a simple wardrobe malfunction. Why else would she be over here in the dark? Waiting to jump you?"

Wes gave him a look and Max gaped. "You lucky bastard. People actually try to ambush you with *in-person* unsolicited nudes?"

Wes sighed. That was pretty much the sort of thing he'd been forced to deal with lately.

His breakup with his longtime girlfriend Gigi had been all over the tabloids and even front page news for one of what he had assumed to be the more respectable papers. Women had been throwing themselves at him for weeks since then. Now he had just made the mistake of assuming an innocent woman was one of the ones who were trying to heal his heart by transplanting his organ into theirs.

He needed to find her and apologize for his rudeness.

He heard a sound at the sliding door and sighed with relief when he saw the woman come back out. He opened his mouth to begin his apology when he suddenly noticed the huge pitcher she was carrying in her hands.

He shut his eyes just in time to be completely drenched in beer.

He heard a horrified gasp from Max and an amused snort from the woman. The beer stung his eyes when he tried to open them and he cursed.

"Asshole," the woman said before he heard her turn on her heel and walk away.

"Well, shit," he heard Max say.

He felt his eyes dabbed with a napkin and Max called a waiter over to help guide him to get cleaned up in the bathroom.

"I'm going to go make sure she isn't giving impromptu showers to anyone else," the man offered before leaving hurriedly.

Three months ago

-

"I promise to not commit murder under any circumstances."

"Great, you can read," Leah said pleasantly to the two adults reading the rules she'd handed them seconds before. "Now try again with no noticeable tone of sarcasm."

Leah was nothing if not safety-conscious.

After the incident with Wes and Mia some months ago, the two of them had gone out of their way to stay away from each other even after Leah had intervened and tried to sort out their initial misunderstanding. Neither of them were having any of it.

Mia was positive Westley was an anthropomorphic sentient dick (who still didn't remember her) and Wes was sure Mia was a short-tempered, unreasonable woman. He wouldn't use stronger words only because his mother had raised him better. He'd tried to apologize and she'd given him such a withering glance that he'd stopped halfway through and simply walked away. She was out of her mind if she thought he would go out of his way to get her to forgive him for a simple misunderstanding.

Even now, it had been months and they never bothered staying in the same breathing space for longer than five minutes if they happened to be in the same room, which for some reason was happening a lot more frequently for some reason.

Mia had made partner at her firm at such a young age and frequently handled clients he worked with himself. Westley wasn't a lawyer but was definitely business savvy and enjoyed watching the woman pointedly ignore him, somehow managing to keep her face neutral when he would ask the most pedantic of questions but answering concisely, each time.

"You two need to get along. *Please*." Leah had said with a sigh as she took a moment to lean against the van she'd parked next to the set-up stall. "I need both of you to help me with this. I'm seriously shorthanded."

Leah was determined that the Fireworks display would go on without a hitch. The Siavonga beachfront area for the event was huge and the actual lighting of the fireworks was being done on a large perfectly flat rock that was located almost three hundred meters from the beach and in the actual water. There was enough room on the rock to hold fifteen men lying down and the low tide had ensured it was almost perfectly dry.

Several boats were in the water a short distance away with first aid kits and life guards. Several more were closer to shore, waiting in case anything happened.

Leah had had a makeshift shed constructed to house the extra fireworks that would be brought out as the night went and she had this put almost fifty meters away from the stall where Wes and Mia were selling the smaller, friendlier fireworks to older children and adults. She'd also been sure to have their stall pretty far from the visitors.

Leah's van was parked pretty close to the stall and the bright words, 'Ellandell Events' was painted neatly onto the side in large letters. Mia always smiled when she said that name. 'Ellandell' was pretty much 'L and L', for Leah and Lehman, her husband.

She hadn't been chosen to organize the local event by herself and after several disagreements, she'd been removed from the planners only to be called at the last minute when the host had argued with her cousin and fired her.

Leah had hustled to get everything ready in just three days and when a young couple had broken up and ditched from the volunteers, she'd had to ask Wes and Mia to help handle the stall. It showed how desperate the situation was.

But it seemed Leah had thought of everything, even the cold. The stall had a few lit braziers at the back that they sat near to get a little warmer once the cold sea air started drifting in.

"Anything can happen," she'd said.

Mia and Wes had somehow managed to stay on opposite ends of the stall in complete silence, only speaking to customers. Leah called Wes over to bring out an extra box of large fireworks so they could be rowed over to Racer's Rock so there would be no lull as they shot them off. Mia had been both pleased and irked when Leah had assured her that Wes didn't remember her and that she hadn't seen fit to enlighten him. Mia thought it meant that she had changed so much he didn't recognize the mousy, shy girl she had been and part of her was grateful for that.

"You left the shed door open," Mia said immediately Wes put the heavy box down. She pointedly ignored the way his shirt stretched across his chest as he did and she turned away, disgusted with herself for noticing how good he looked in a simple t-shirt and jeans.

"It got stuck in the sand. Maybe a stone or something. It wouldn't budge," he said, giving her a dark look. "And this box is pretty heavy."

Mia shrugged as she took the money from the twelve year old that'd walked all the way to them to get some sparklers and a box of the smaller fireworks.

"Would you please light a sparkler up for me?" he asked politely.

"Sure thing," Mia gave him a warm smile and the boy blushed. Wes almost rolled his eyes at the pre-teen but he could see the appeal as Mia bent over to grab the box of matches she'd just dropped.

She removed one sparkler and grabbed the box of fireworks before she turned to Wes who was still standing there as she lit it.

"Aren't you going to go close the shed door?" she asked. "It's not safe leaving it open like that."

"I'll get to it," he said through gritted teeth.

She was right and he had been about to go close it but he wasn't interested in going if she was going to nag.

"Why can't you go now?"

"What exactly is your problem?" he asked, irritably. "Why don't you just get it out of your system?"

He thought she'd turn away but-

"You thought I was a *prostitute*," she said immediately.

"You were dressed like one." He didn't even bother pointing out that it had been months ago and she should get over it.

"My dress *ripped*. That was an accident," she hissed.

"You threw your drink at me," he responded.

"There was barely anything left in my glass," she scoffed.

"You came back with a pitcher of beer and threw that at me, too."

Mia smiled. "Yeah... good times."

Wes looked somewhat impressed. "Wow, you're crazy."

Mia's brown eyes narrowed. "*Excuse me?*"

Wes raised an eyebrow in challenge. "You heard me."

Crazy.

It was something Eric usually called her – especially right before he broke up with her. There were times they'd make plans and on the day of their dates or outings, Eric would say he hadn't asked her or that she'd said a different date. Or even that he hadn't agreed to it. She'd taken to recording their conversations when she made the plans for her own peace of mind and when Eric denied ever agreeing to one movie date, she played him the recording.

She'd thought he would apologize or at least say he had forgotten.

Instead, he'd called her behavior pathetic and said if she *really* wanted to go, they could. When she insisted he admit he was wrong, he'd said maybe they shouldn't be around each other so much. It was making her crazy – what with the recording him and all.

Mia had let it go but he'd still left that time.

Leah said Eric was gaslighting her and that Mia for some reason, knew it but wouldn't let go.

Mia had just gotten back with him the month before and he was already acting irritable and distant again. No doubt he would leave again and soon.

It was that more than the actual word itself that set her off. "How

dare you assume you know *anything* about me or-"

"I know enough," Westley said in a bored tone.

"You don't know *anything*," she said, her voice dangerously low.

At the last word, the sparkler in her fist broke in two and she glared

at him.

Wes was perfectly content to glare right back.

"Um…" they both turned to look at the boy but he was staring at

the ground near them.

That was when they noticed the hissing sound.

"Crap."

In her anger, she'd dropped the box of fireworks onto the ground

and one end had caught fire on the brazier.

Mia tried to grab the box but Wes pulled her away just in time. One

of the fuses had already lit and they saw it shoot, box and all, a whole fifty

metres away, directly into the open storage shed.

They both cursed loudly.

"Get to the van," he ordered Mia, pulling her along. He grabbed the boy and the three of them ran off toward the van. Wes pretty much threw Mia and the kid into the van and shut the door behind them as they heard the explosions go off in the makeshift storage shed.

The fireworks went off for what seemed to be a ten minutes and they heard excited screams and yells from the crowd.

Eventually they got out and the boy's mother came racing toward them, clutching at her child and cradling him, thanking them for protecting him and keeping him safe.

Leah and Max jogged up to them as the fire department arrived and took care of the rest, still keeping the crowd a good distance away in case any more went off. Luckily they were far enough that most of the crowd had assumed it was part of the show.

"What happened?" Leah asked after making sure they were both alright.

Wes and Mia looked at each other and immediately started placing the blame on the other party.

Leah groaned as Max laughed. "You owe me five dollars."

One month ago.

-

Leah swore under her breath when she saw Wes and Mia pause in front of each other.

"Calm down," her husband said, giving her a quick squeeze as he stood by her. "They're adults."

Leah gave Lehman an unsure glance and he shrugged. "If they set the place on fire, at least it's not our house."

At his wife's sharp glare, he gave her a sheepish smile and she rolled her eyes at him and let him kiss her cheek.

She had made sure to invite Wes and Mia to the fundraising dinner at different times. Early enough that Mia would fulfill her social duties and get back to her office before Wes showed up.

Wes was early.

Leah walked toward them to get started on any damage control.

"You haven't changed a bit," Mia said with a tight smile.

"I take it you mean that you still think I'm an asshole," Wes replied, with a bored tone. He'd had a long day and wasn't feeling up to the challenge of riling her up, even for his own amusement.

"Pretty much, yes."

"Did you ever doubt me?" he asked.

"There was a while it was up in the air."

He chuckled despite himself. "I'm glad I lived up to your expectations."

Mia gave him a mirthless smile. "You should be proud."

They spoke as politely as they could for a few minutes before they realized everyone was watching them warily.

"You burn down a storage shed *one time*..." Mia muttered.

Wes smothered a chuckle.

"Hello, Friends," Leah said, coming up to them. "I do hope you're both behaving."

"Of course," Mia said immediately giving her friend a reassuring smile. Wes could feel the warmth in that smile and wondered if she would ever have given him one if they hadn't had that disastrous first meeting.

Leah turned to Westley and he smiled charmingly. "It's true. We haven't tried to kill each other at all. We'll fit that in later."

"Not funny," Leah said with a ferocious glare. Westley and Mia both stifled their laughter. Leah was small and adorable, especially when she was angry.

"Tell you what, we may even share a dance," Wes said.

"Ha," Mia snorted.

She caught Leah giving her a pleading look and she sighed. "I mean... yes. A dance. Lovely idea."

Westley offered her his hand and Mia took it.

"I see your gown covers you right up this time," Wes said and he led her to the dance floor.

"I'm glad you approve," Mia replied, turning to face him as if displaying herself for his perusal. He took her up on her unspoken offer.

Her big coily hair was pulled up in a neat, gel-sleeked pineapple with some strands curled and hanging to the sides of her face. It made her light brown eyes seem even larger. Her midnight dress with a halter top that covered her chest completely, and went all the way to the floor, exposed only her arms and her back. She looked good in it and she knew it – though he did see a glimmer of unease in her eyes before she steeled herself and raised a challenging eyebrow at him.

Wes rested his hand on Mia's lower back and smiled devilishly when he felt her shiver. She was a full-bodied woman – hips, thighs, ass, breasts…

There was something to hold onto on every part of her and Westley cleared his throat.

"Leah told me she'd really hoped we would get along," Wes said. "That first night she'd planned to introduce us."

Mia remembered Leah mentioning something like that to her. "I imagine it would have gone just as badly," she said, following his lead effortlessly as they danced.

"I think you're right. Besides," Wes spun them around and smiled that arrogant smile of his, pulling her closer. "You're just not my type."

Mia looked up at him and smiled slowly, catching him off guard. She took the opportunity to press her body closer to him so he could feel every curve. Without breaking eye contact, she whispered, "Say that when I can't feel your boner against my thigh."

She abruptly pulled away from him and with a polite nod, left the dance-floor.

At the bar, Max handed a ten dollar bill to Leah.

"I was sure they'd do more damage," he complained.

Leah gave him an amused glance and turned back in time to see the hint of a smile on Wes' face as he watched Mia go.

-

Recipe for Heartbreak

- ¾ cup flour
- ½ cup cocoa powder
- 1 cup sugar
- 2 large eggs
- 1 teaspoon vanilla essence
- ¼ teaspoon salt
- ¼ teaspoon baking powder
- Chocolate bar of your choice
- Milk

- ➢ Preheat the oven to 175 degrees Celsius.
- ➢ Grease a square pan.
- ➢ Melt chocolate bar in milk.
- ➢ Mix everything else.
- ➢ Mix with your melted chocolate.
- ➢ Bake for 20 to 25 minutes.

Note: Best consumed during the last weeks of spring while a magazine with beautiful, young, skinny models on nearly every page (except for that one page with the skinny old lady – something about Alzheimer's) asks you if your body is ready for summer.

- Realize you don't need him.
- Forget what you realized.
- Cry.
- Stand on a scale.
- Eat more brownies.
- Take your time.

Chapter 1: Recipe for Heartbreak

Present day

"Eric said *what*?" Leah screamed into the phone.

Mia pulled the phone away from her ear and turned back to her paperwork, going over it to make sure she hadn't written something Leah had said as they spoke.

"He said we need a break," Mia said, rearranging her papers again. "And that I should use our time apart to 'work on myself'. He left a gym membership pamphlet and some diet pill brochures."

Leah swore like a sailor before she took in a deep breath.

"Are you alright?"

Mia nodded even though her friend couldn't see her. "Yeah. It's temporary. I'm sure he just feels neglected and-"

"Mia, honey… Why do you keep putting up with this? He does this *all the time*! He insults you. He degrades you. And then he goes off for weeks or months and when he's done seeing other women like some sort of *vaginal investigator*, he comes right back and you're right there waiting! And he *knows* you're there waiting!"

Mia bit her lip.

She wasn't *waiting*. Technically.

She lived with him. That was her apartment, too.

Where was she supposed to go?

Whenever they went on a break, he would move out for weeks, sometimes months, not taking any of his things with him.

Yes, it was frustrating. It wasn't fair he was going off doing who knew what and he would come back and like an idiot, she always took him back.

Always.

She was a creature of habit and…

…and she was scared she had made this a habit.

If it had been anyone else, she would have told them off for accepting that sort of behavior.

He was disrespecting her. He was using her. He was an asshole.

But why couldn't she let him go?

Leah sighed on the phone and talked to someone in the background. "I have to go, honey," she said to Mia.

Mia said goodbye and called her secretary to cancel everything else she'd had for the rest of the day. She left early and went back home.

She opened her apartment door and called out.

No answer.

What had she been expecting?

She went into the bedroom and sat down heavily on the bed.

Pictures of her and Eric were all over the wall. With his boyish face, sandy hair, hazel eyes… he was your typical boy next door. Sweet and attractive. You'd never know he was a famous artist. Maybe that was what she liked, the spontaneity of him.

They'd met in college and had been dating on and off since then. Almost seven years by her count while she wondered if he even counted any. Leah was right. Eric sometimes asked for a break without a warning.

Mia always thought they were happy and everything was fine and he always managed to pull the rug from under her.

She stared at the ceiling, running the previous night through her mind.

She couldn't figure out what had happened, or why she'd let it happen at all but she hated the question that kept running through her head.

Did I do something wrong?

She had found a beautiful black lingerie set on their bed and thought it was a gift, though it didn't fit her well.

Eric had walked in late to find her trying it on and had snickered, telling her of course it wouldn't fit – it wasn't in *her* size.

And he'd left a note on where to return it but when she checked, it wasn't the address for a store.

Her only comfort was it was new so she hadn't worn some other woman's teddy though she *had* probably stretched it out quite a bit.

And she shouldn't have felt vindictive in knowing that he was *still* going to give it to whatever woman he was seeing now.

Because he was.

She knew he was.

Mia hugged a pillow to herself and breathed in his scent, cursing herself.

"Mia?"

Mia jumped and almost fell off the bed.

"Leah, damn it, you scared me!"

Leah smiled apologetically and lifted the bag in her hands. Chinese food.

"Your secretary said I'd just missed you," Leah set the food down and walked over to the bed. She took the pillow away from her friend and put her head in her lap. She started to stroke her hair, not saying anything.

Mia sniffed. "You didn't have to come."

"I know."

She buried her face into Leah's lap. "I'm fine, really."

"I know."

She dug her fingernails into her palms and bit her lip as the tears flowed freely. "Why does he always leave me?"

"I don't know," Leah said softly.

She let Mia cry until she was exhausted and all that were left were shakes. She then gently forced her to eat.

"What do you want to do?" Leah asked as Mia dug into the reheated dumplings.

"I don't want to be here moping," Mia said sheepishly. "I'm tired of him doing this."

Leah gave her an encouraging but tired smile that spoke volumes. They'd had this conversation before. "Do you want him back?"

Mia nodded miserably but said, "But that's to be expected. I don't want to, though."

Leah bit her lip. "Um, I'm going to suggest something and I need you to hear me out, okay?"

Mia looked at her warily and Leah laughed. "Come on, I'm your best friend. I only have your best interests at heart."

"Okay, shoot."

"Do you really want him back?"

"Right now, I do, yes. But… I'm tired of him treating me like crap."

"Okay," Leah said. "I think you need to get out of here first."

"What?"

"This apartment," she clarified. "It has all your memories, all your stuff. He's someplace that has no reminder of you at all. You need to leave."

"I can't stay with you-" Mia started to say with a frown.

Leah shut her up with a glance. "First of all, yes you can. Second, that's not what I'm suggesting. I'm thinking you need a new environment. You know, help you think and clear your head."

Mia nodded slowly. "Okay… I can't leave work either."

"Yes, you can. But again, not what I mean. They can afford to send your snail mail to another address for about six months."

"That's an oddly specific amount of time."

Leah had the decency to look guilty. "I have news."

"You're pregnant?"

She got slapped for that.

Leah grinned. "I am officially the Event planner for our country's A to Z branch. Well, I'm on probation but…"

Mia gaped and then grinned and hugged her friend. "Congratulations! That's huge!"

The A to Z was a huge corporation whose fingers were in every honeypot. From producing reality game shows, pop stars, superhero movies, anime to owning supermarkets wholefoods and, to hear people tell it, the Earth. A to Z was a household name.

"I'm glad you're happy for me," Leah said with a grin.

"Why wouldn't I be?" Mia asked, a sudden feeling of foreboding springing up.

"I'm glad you realize *how much* I need this," Lead added.

"No," Mia said preemptively.

"Too late. You owe me for almost wrecking my last event."

"What? People loved it. They said it was amazing how you'd had the presence of mind to have a land-level fireworks display. They called you a *genius*."

"As is my due," Leah shrugged. "But it could've gone very wrong."

Mia was openly scowling at her friend's obvious manipulation. "I said I was sorry."

"Someone could have died."

"I get it-"

"I could have gone into labour because of the shock."

"You said you're not pregnant."

"My periods started early because of the stress you caused me."

Mia sighed. "What do you want?"

"Whatever it is," Leah gave her an innocent smile. "I want you to know that I only did this because I love you. I signed you up after you called me."

"What? To what?"

"You remember George?"

Mia thought for a moment. "The real estate guy?"

Leah chuckled. "You mean the *owner* of the RR real estate company."

Mia rolled her eyes. "Yeah, him."

"Yes," Leah smiled. "Well, his company made a program to cater to smaller buyers and renters. You know, people looking for roommates or housemates."

"You want me to get a roommate?"

"No. You're a grown ass woman," Leah snorted. "I mean a house mate. I don't want you wallowing on your own and calling Eric every other day to see if he took his allergy medicine. You're not his mother."

Mia looked away guiltily, knowing Leah knew her a little too well.

Leah put a hand on her friend's knee, "I already signed you up. This is a trial program and George has a lot at stake. If it works, they're actually thinking of advertising it by using a TV show with housemates put together based on their compatibility."

"That sounds like a dating show. Or a show that already exists. Or both."

"It does but no. They want to run the show as a publicity stunt and free advertising for their services in finding ideal housemates for a good price. You're not part of the show trial, don't worry. You're part of the actual housemates program."

"Won't I be biased because you're my friend?"

"Don't you dare. We need to know if it's viable so lying won't help me. You're the only person I could get on such short notice who could actually afford the bracket we want. We have several homes for different income brackets and there was one left."

"I don't know…"

"Let's check it out first. It's probably cheaper than all your impulse buys. But if you really don't like it, I'll go find someone else to grovel to," Leah said.

"You're not going to give me any time to think this through are you?"

"I'm trying not to. You'll end up staying here and being miserable," Leah said. "Look, the lease is only for six months and the program's been proven to match you perfectly to your housemate."

"Wait, I can't meet them before? What if they're killers or weird or-"

"George would be out of business if he let anything like that slide by him. The people get interviewed. He has them investigated thoroughly. Also, would I let you go get murdered?"

"If it would keep me away from Eric?"

"Good answer but no."

Mia sighed and Leah nudged her. "Just think about it. Do you really want to still be waiting here when Eric is done with his other women?"

Mia bit her lip, feeling the familiar anger of the last three times Eric had done this.

No.

She didn't want to wait for him like someone who had no other option.

She didn't want to feel like she was worthless anymore.

She knew Leah meant well but she also knew her friend would support her, whatever her decision.

She put herself in Leah's shoes. Watching your friend accept someone treating them like garbage had to be difficult. If Lehman had even dared try that with Leah, Mia would have been the first person packing her friend's shit.

Enough was enough.

"What do I have to do?" she asked.

Leah squealed and grabbed her, hugging her tightly. "Thank you!"

Mia sighed. "Doesn't seem like I have much of a choice."

"You do but you wouldn't abandon me in my time of need. It starts next week."

Mia groaned. "Why do you keep getting these last minute jobs?"

"Lady Luck… or my husband is sabotaging my competition while I'm not looking. The company that was going to do it was Ever PR. Their rep got food poisoning two hours before their meeting with A to Z and apparently spent a long time in the bathroom before getting the strength to leave. They got stuck in the worst traffic jam. Then the replacement they sent got lost and the back up's back up broke his leg and was rushed to hospital. The A to Z manager was livid at being stood up and refused to take any calls explaining the situation. When he did hear them out, it all sounded too ridiculous."

"Wow."

"Yeah. Tough for them but good for me.," Leah grinned.

Leah took her to meet George that evening. George was a pleasant man in his fifties and welcomed them both warmly.

"Good afternoon, ladies," he said with a smile.

They shook hands and Leah took over the conversation.

Mia was sure her friend had briefed George on her immediate need for a place.

George nodded when Leah was done explaining what sort of area Mia would prefer.

"So you would like the Housemate Hunter package," he said thoughtfully, before he walked over to his desk. "I'll need you to just fill in some forms and we can have a place ready for you by next week."

"That quick, huh?" Mia asked and George nodded.

"There are always places ready to be occupied and I can think of five suitable ones off the top of my head. Many people are looking for house mates to cut costs or for safety or practical reasons. It's much easier to find and match them based on these tests. We also cross-reference and check your details with the police departments, banks, old neighbours…"

"Wow," Mia chuckled. "That's pretty thorough."

"You get what you pay for," he said with a grin.

Mia chuckled. "Alright, where's this test then?"

George had an iPad brought to her and he chatted with Leah while Mia filled in the forms. After promising to get back to her within a week, Mia went back home, refusing Leah's offer to stay with her.

After ten minutes of staring at the pictures on the walls, Mia packed two large suitcases with her clothes and called Leah.

It was just a week till she'd be out and she wasn't ready to spend it being reminded of him every day.

***

"It's perfect!" Mia said excitedly as she and Leah toured the place George had found for her. Leah laughed as Mia started pointing out where she would rearrange the furniture and which room she'd choose.

She thought she'd let her housemate have the bigger room as a show of good faith in the hopes they'd get along.

"Will you need time to think about it?" George asked once the women were done squealing at the prospect of redecorating a new place.

"No, no, I want it!" Mia said, wrapping herself around a pillar. The house was a modern, gray, open space rectangular building. The grass at the back was neatly cut and there was a pool and a garden off to the side with tomatoes, onions and lettuce already growing there. Mia had fallen in love with it the moment they'd driven up to it.

George laughed and handed her the lease forms. "Initially it's for six months and-"

Mia listened politely but she'd already read the terms and conditions. The housemates would sign the agreement to rent the place for six months because it was a new program and George didn't want people flaking on it. She thought it seemed fair.

"So when do I meet my new housemate?" she asked after she'd signed it. She'd already read that he was male; something she'd said she didn't mind. He was a workaholic, liked to keep to himself, wouldn't be loud or overbearing, had good credit, no criminal record and was twenty-nine years old.

His name and face were withheld but George had assured her that was just something he liked to do.

It was weird since she had all that other information, including his blood type (O positive) and favourite colour (green) but she didn't push it.

George said her housemate would be moving in a week after her and that he would be there to introduce them. If the man made her uncomfortable in any way or seemed like a creep, he would find her another one.

-

Recipe for Disaster

- 5 fresh lemons from the Whole Foods section of the supermarket (be sure to hide the bag from the woman who sells fruit down the street. Use another route to get home)
- Three tablespoons of salt (you will need but a dash)
- Human hand (preferably your own, still attached)
- 1 bottle Tequila
- Saliva

> Slice the lemons in thin or thick wedges
> Wet the back of your hand with the liquid of your choice (flavoured water or saliva, whichever is available at the time)
> Pour a dash of salt onto the skin of your wet hand being careful not to miss
> Lick the moistened salt off of your hand
> Drink the tequila
> Quickly bite into the lemon wedge.

Note: Best served post-breakup in the presence of non-judgmental female college students who will tell you you are beautiful and that they love your shoes.

Chapter 2: Recipe for Disaster

-

Mia and Westley stared at each other for a full minute before Westley muttered, "I really should have seen this coming."

Mia turned to glare at the widely grinning George and slightly apologetic looking Leah.

"I will sue you both for everything you have," Mia said to them.

"Feel free to take my firstborn," George said pleasantly. "Lord knows my wife holds on tightly to everything else. Besides, you read through everything and as a lawyer, I'm sure you saw it's iron-clad."

Mia couldn't argue with that. It was.

"You tricked us," Westley said.

"Really? Did I lie at any point?" George replied. "It was a surprise to me, too," he added. "But no one else was more suitably matched to share a house than you two. An eighty-six percent match."

"We might burn the place down," Westley said, taking a step back as if inspecting how flammable the ceiling was.

"That's true," Mia said. "I think you should find me another housemate."

"Yes." Westley paused. "Or another house. I like this one."

"I was here first," Mia said, crossing her arms.

Wes snorted. "Did you plant your flag and everything? Claim the house as a sovereign nation?"

"I'll plant my flag up your -"

"Children, please."

Mia turned to whine at the only person who she thought could help her, "*Leah!*"

Leah raised her hands, placating. "It's just six months. Besides, you both already paid and you know how George feels about giving money back to people. "

George's refund policy was clearly written on the contracts as '*Over my cold, dead body*'.

"Fine," Mia said before she turned to Westley. "I'm not leaving."

Wes had been perfectly willing to try be reasonable and maybe find a new place to stay first thing in the morning but when that meant giving in and letting this woman have her way, there was no way in hell he was going to go anywhere.

"Oh? Then I guess you have a new housemate because I'm not leaving, either."

Mia groaned inwardly. She should have offered to leave. Hell, she should have just left. But that would have meant that he'd won! That he'd managed to chase her out of her new fort!

The two glared at each other and then went off to their separate rooms.

Mia was already regretting having let her new housemate have the bigger bedroom.

At least both were self-contained and she wouldn't have to worry about sharing a bathroom with him.

George and Leah left soon after when it was clear the two adults were apparently sulking in their rooms.

***

Max met Mia for lunch that day and she explained everything.

"You mean to tell me you're living with a sex god," Max asked slowly. "And you're *complaining*?"

The hot waiter serving them brought their drinks and Max turned to him with a bitter expression on his face. "*You're* attractive. Are you *also* going to shack up with my friend here?"

"I'm gay," the waiter replied. "But I would watch your sex tape," he added to Mia who raised her glass to him in thanks.

Max blinked in surprise. Was his gaydar slacking?

"I'm Max and I too am of The Gay," Max said, fluttering his lashes at the waiter. "What time do you get off?"

"When you get me off?" the man replied with a wink.

Max grinned widely, letting his gaze sweep over the man he had every intention of riding like a racehorse in fifteen minutes. "I'm going to leave you a *huge tip* when my friend here is done whining about her glorious life and then you're going to show me where the bathroom is because I will get lost on my way there if I attempt to find it on my own."

The waiter nodded. "Let me know when you need it."

Max bit his lip as the man left. "Oh, I will *break* him."

Mia rolled her eyes and Max turned back to her with an earnest expression. "You have my undivided attention for the next ten to fifteen minutes. So what do you want to do about the house? Leave?"

"No!" she frowned. "I want *him* to leave!"

Max smiled slowly, mischievously. "You want to chase the man out of his own home?"

"Yes," she replied, unashamed.

Max grinned. "Then just be a nightmare to live with. Always works for me."

"And your commitment issues?"

"I don't have commitment issues. I just get bored easily."

Mia raised her eyebrow at that and he stared back at her, unblinking. "What?"

She shook her head at him and wondered if that would be the answer. If all she had to do was try get rid of him, that could be pretty easy.

***

Mia got home pretty early after lunch with Max and sighed as she dug out her keys and opened the door.

Or tried to.

She turned the key and tried again.

It didn't budge.

Frowning, Mia looked at her set of keys and tried another.

Nothing happened.

She stared at the door and then at her keys.

And then she heard it…

A loud laugh coming from the other side of the door.

She went around the house and tried the back door even though she knew it would pretty much be the same story.

Westley had changed the locks on all the doors.

"You asshole!" she yelled.

More laughter greeted her.

**

The locksmith had been pretty surprised to be back so soon and cutting keys for Mia but he'd been forced to hurry back when Mia had threatened to sue him.

Westley had been sure she would have keyed his car but it had been safely in the two-door garage and she had been locked out of that, too.

Mia parked her black Porsche next to Westley's blue Ferrari and resisted the urge to key his car. It was beautiful and it would be *such* a shame if anything were to happen to it…

She finally opened the door that led into the house from the garage and she sighed with relief when she got in.

Westley had had to pay the locksmith again when she'd refused to and he'd braced himself for an argument.

Mia however, caught on quick and after throwing him a dirty look, had simply gone off to her room. He was trying to annoy her into leaving but now she *definitely* wasn't going anywhere.

For three days, Mia did nothing and Westley had started to relax. He got up in the middle of the night to get a glass of water from the kitchen, a habit he'd never once broken even after moving to the new house.

"FUCKING HELL!"

Mia chuckled to herself, smiling at the memory of all the Legos she'd strewn across the floor to the kitchen. She fell asleep to the sound of more cursing as Westley hopped in the dark unwittingly from one Lego piece to another and then, from the loud sound she heard after, promptly just fell to the ground onto the rest.

It seemed the dam had broken on the lives of two once perfectly reasonable adults.

Mia found her bed wrapped in layers of foil that simply hid layers of plastic wrap. Westley found he couldn't get to work on time because someone had apparently thrown a party for all the dogs from the animal shelter on their driveway. The dogs refused to move out of the way and the photographers and children were saying how great the whole thing was.

Mia opened the door to a house filled with balloons with a random number of them popping as she waded through and Westley found that he'd been ordered a fully paid-for performance by some retired strippers who were now well-seasoned octogenarians. He hadn't had the heart to insist they put their clothes back on and stop trying to do splits. He was saved when one of them threw out her back and he had to call 911.

Mia and Wes had barely shared the house for two weeks.

On their ninth day together, Mia came home from work to find a post-it stuck on a black satchel hanging from the doorknob. She narrowed her eyes at it in suspicion.

"I feel like this is a fair way to sort out our current differences. I have some balloons and you have some balloons. They are filled with paint. When the clock strikes six, I will attack."

Mia stared at the note and then held one of the paint filled balloons in her hands.

He wouldn't dare.

She spotted a shoe peeking out from the corner of the garage and she frowned, looking at her watch. Five minutes to six.

She put down her bag and took off her shoes. There was no way she would let him ruin those.

There was also the fact that she had no intention of playing his stupid game. She picked up the satchel; ready to throw it away when a sudden splash in front of her splattered her feet in red.

She saw Westley grinning challengingly.

He'd missed on purpose. But he would hit her whether she decided to defend herself or not. Mia grabbed the satchel and backed away as he smirked.

Fine.

She'd play his stupid game.

There was no way she'd lose but of course, she hadn't accounted for Westley cheating.

***

Thirty minutes later, Mia and Westley were sitting on the front lawn, covered in red paint and looking back stubbornly at the police officer who was standing and lecturing the two of them.

Apparently one of their neighbours had seen 'someone chasing someone else who was covered in blood'.

The officer had been closest and luckily, found the two of them even before any backup had decided to go along and help.

57

"It's just paint," Mia said, cutting off his unbearably long lecture. Why he was telling them about the dangers of faking a murder, she didn't understand.

"Yes, I can see that. I went to college. I know what paint is."

Mia and Wes shared a glance.

"You cannot go around being a public nuisance."

"We were in our own yard and-

"Your neighbours are old women. Old, gossiping women. They see all, they know all, they have been calling us *every day* since you two moved here and we actually thought there might be something real this time."

"Um…" Westley looked serious. "I'm sorry you didn't find the homicide you were hoping for."

The officer released a put-upon sigh. "Yeah, me too."

"This won't happen again," Mia assured him.

"Be that as it may, I'll have to report this to Mr. George."

They blinked. "What? What for?"

"Don't worry, it's standard practice," he said and then with a wicked grin, added. "But keep in mind that the man can be petty and he can make sure you never find a good place to stay. Ever."

Westley snorted. "All a real estate agent requires is money."

The officer laughed drily. "That's what they thought, too."

"Who?"

"The people who lived here before you."

"Where are they now?" Wes asked carefully.

"Trailer park on the outskirts of town."

"Did they fall on hard times?"

"Not even." He replied with a sharp grin. "They just irritated George."

The officer left and George arrived minutes later with a lecture of his own.

He sat with them both and rubbed at the wrinkles forming between his eyes. "You cannot change the locks on the doors and you cannot host a *dog* party around his car-"

"*Puppy* party."

He sighed. "…Puppy party, so he's late for work."

"I regret nothing," Mia said.

"Don't forget the landmines," Wes muttered.

"They were Legos."

Both men looked at her like actual landmines would have been preferable.

George kept berating them for almost a whole hour and Mia slipped off of the chair and onto her knees. "Your lecture is too long. Please, I have a family."

George gave her a very serious look and Westley sighed. "What she means is we are very sorry."

Mia nodded. "Very, *very* sorry."

George nodded after giving them both some extra threats. "If you make any more trouble for me, it won't be pleasant."

They nodded.

"You both came here for your own personal reasons but this is my livelihood. I don't take kindly to people playing with my work, no matter how rich they are."

Both of them gave him innocent smiles and he stood and left them without another word.

They waved him off happily and smiled wider at their nosy old neighbours as soon as George was gone. Mrs. Bwalya and the redundantly named Old Widow Wamasiye turned away from them with clear suspicion in their eyes.

"I can't believe they called the cops on us," Mia said as Westley shut the door.

"Maybe they really did think we were trying to murder each other."

"That's no reason to call the police."

Westley chuckled and then paused, giving her a strange look, like he was trying to figure her out.

She knew that if she were a lesser woman, she would have melted under his scrutiny. However, both of them were covered in caked-up red paint and looked like they'd been on the losing side of a war.

"What?" she asked.

"George said we both had our personal reasons for coming to stay here. I won't pry into yours and will assume you'll do the same. He's right, though, I *do* need to stay here."

"You have enough money to buy a home in another country," Mia said. "You could just leave."

Westley shrugged. "Can't. I have my reasons."

Mia hesitated and Westley looked away uncomfortably for a moment.

He sighed and said, "Look, we got off to a bad start-"

She scoffed and he gave a tiny boyish smile. "*Several* bad starts," he amended. "I'd apologize but you wouldn't take it seriously."

He was right.

Mia nodded. "Well, I would apologize, too, but I think it was entirely your fault."

Westley laughed at that, blue eyes bright with humour. "Fine. Stubborn woman."

She raised an elegant eyebrow at him and he held out his hand.

"It's only six months. Truce?"

Mia felt the familiar anger and irritation that he barely remembered her at all from that meeting that had grown her loathing for him. She supposed it might not have been a big deal to him but it had been to her.

But…

But she needed to stay there just as much, if not more, than he did.

Mia sighed and grudgingly took his offered hand. "Truce."

-

Recipe for Forgiveness

- 10 fresh lemons
- 1 cup Salt
- 1 bottle Tequila (unfinished)

- ➤ Slice the lemons in half
- ➤ Replace the salt with sugar
- ➤ Replace the tequila with water (hot and cold)
- ➤ Dissolve the sugar in hot water. Then add ice cold water.
- ➤ Squeeze those lemons. Collect juice in jar.
- ➤ Stir sweetened water and lemon juice.

Note: Double check that you have not used Tequila in the recipe.

- Drink lemonade.
- Listen to Lemonade.
- Take frequent bathroom breaks.

-

Chapter 3: Recipe for Forgiveness

-

It was Saturday morning and Mia was *starving*.

It had been three days since she and Westley had agreed to their truce and both of them got the idea that staying out of each other's way and essentially never seeing each other was the best way to not end up in a trailer park. Or prison.

So far it had been three days of her skirting around the house after hearing him come and go. She had heard him leave his room but hadn't heard any of the doors leading outside open or close. He was definitely in the house, but where?

She had been working diligently, expecting him to leave or return to his room so she could go make herself a sandwich but whatever room he was in, he wasn't budging.

She decided it was worth the risk and left her room for the kitchen.

Mia blinked.

Nothing in the fridge had moved.

She supposed Westley was something of a half-decent housemate if he never touched her stuff or replaced everything but she did recall that she'd eaten the last of her yogurt and the take-out she'd carried from Friday didn't smell quite right.

Everything was in its place but none of it was edible. Margarine, jam, sauces…

Mia rummaged through the fridge, mumbling things under her breath. She had forgotten to get more bread and cheese and there was only half an onion and some tomatoes Leah had brought them. There was no ham or sweet meats and she decided to do without.

"A tomato salad then?" she said to herself, hyping up what was to be some seasoned cheese-lacking tomatoes.

She wasn't much of a cook and ignored the beef, chicken and turkey in the freezer and defrosted lamb in the fridge. It would be best if she didn't burn the house down.

She sighed and took a large tomato out and washed it. She sat on a barstool at the island in the middle of the room and grabbed herself a knife. She sliced it up and salted it before plopping a slice into her mouth.

Mia heard the kitchen door slide open and paused, looking up.

Westley looked at her with an amused expression on his face. She tried her best to keep her own face expressionless.

He looked way too good in his sweatpants and vest with his hair messy and the slightest hint of dark circles under his eyes.

He stepped into the room and leaned against the counter. "I was wondering why none of the food was really being touched. Is that all you've been eating?"

Mia sniffed imperiously, salting another slice and eating it. She didn't miss the way his eyes followed the slice. "Leah brought us some tomatoes."

"Nice of her." He said before pointedly looking at the large tomato in her hand that was halfway gone. "You know, if you're going to have rabbit food, you should at least have an actual salad."

Mia looked like she wanted to say something extremely rude but thought better of it. "We're out of lettuce."

Westley walked to the large two-door fridge, opened the bottom vegetable compartment and pulled out a head of lettuce. "There's more in the garden outside. How do you usually feed yourself?"

Mia's face burned and she looked away, muttering, "I order out but the places I usually order from don't deliver here." When she was at the office, she often carried home leftovers from her takeout and ate that.

Westley seemed to study her for a moment before it occurred to him that Mia probably had no idea where anything was. It was likely that she was a workaholic and lived off of take-out or cup ramen.

He was amused, she could tell, so she kept purposefully eating her tomato and he sighed.

"Would you like some mashed potatoes? I always make too much for one person," Westley offered, and Mia knew he was trying to preserve both of their pride.

Mia looked at him in surprise before turning away. "I suppose...if you make too much... We probably shouldn't waste anything..."

It was to his credit that he managed to not roll his eyes and started going through cupboards and pulling out pots and pans. Mia decided she'd come back later and label all the drawers and cupboards so she'd at least know where to get what.

Westley placed a chopping board, knife and some green beans in front of Mia. "Chop those up."

If he thought the woman would argue, he was sorely mistaken. Mia could be exceedingly civil when she needed to eat.

"So…" he said, making conversation as he peeled some potatoes. "Is cooking not your forte or were you too lazy to actually make something?"

"A little of both," she said, chopping expertly. Her skills with a knife belied her lack of them with a stove. "My cooking once killed a man."

Westley laughed and held out a box to her. "Here, snack on some crackers while you sit and look hungry."

She was going to protest but her stomach grumbled. She grumbled right along with it as she grabbed the box of crackers he'd taken from a cupboard and offered to her.

69

"I must warn you," he said, "I'm an amazing cook and it'll start to smell heavenly but I'll need you to be strong."

Mia snorted but thirty minutes later, with the scent of rosemary, thyme and butter wafting off of the lamb roast, she splayed her front over the counter as she watched him mash the potatoes, adding cream, pepper and a spoonful of olive oil.

"Is it ready *now*?" she moaned. "I'm *starving*. It smells ready. Is it *ready*?"

She knew Westley has already told her three times that no, it wasn't ready and he hesitated with his hand on the masher as if he was wondering whether he should use it on her instead.

"Go away; I'll call you when it's ready. Take your crackers with you."

Mia glared but took the crackers and stomped out of the room. She popped her head back in a moment later.

"You *better* call me."

Westley chuckled at her hanger and continued making their meal.

He called her a short while after that and when she immediately came through the door, he realized that she had been standing there, waiting.

"That's creepy. You realize that?"
She gave him a look and proceeded to return to her seat on the island. A large plate had already been set out there and her mouth watered. Roasted lamb, mash and gravy, and a salad with slices of tomato she was positive he was using to mock her…

His plate was opposite hers but instead of sitting down, he picked it up.

"Are you eating in your room?" she asked, unable to hide the small note of curiosity in her voice.

"No, TV room. Would you like to join me? I think the silence would be less awkward if we played something into it."

Mia nodded, picking up her plate and cutlery and having a moment of sadness at not yet having dug into anything.

She followed him to the TV room and sat on the opposite end of the couch. The only other chair available was the uncomfortable looking rigid one George had sat in as he sucked their lives away with his boring words. Westley turned on the TV and flipped to Saturday cartoons. Mia approved but had no interest in voicing that.

She cut easily into the lamb and took a bite.

"Oh my *gosh*."

She hadn't even realized her eyes were closed until she heard, "That good, huh?"

Brown eyes sprang open and met blue.

He had a pleased smile on his face and there was something else there.

She gave him a smile of her own and turned her eyes back to her plate. When she'd eaten enough bites to confirm that it wasn't a fluke or just starvation influencing her taste buds, she looked up at him appreciatively.

"Can you clean as well?"

He nodded. "And do taxes."

"Impressive. Someone will pay at least half a horse in dowry for these skills of yours."

He looked offended. "*Half* a horse? My skills are worth at least two horses *and* a pregnant goat."

Mia laughed and he muttered to himself about her underestimating his worth. They finished the rest of their meal with only the noise from the TV but it wasn't as awkward a silence as it should have been. It was pleasant, companionable.

Mia took their dishes when he was done and set about cleaning up the kitchen. There wasn't much to do as it seemed Wes cleaned as he cooked, pots and all.

He sat at the centre island and had some juice, letting her dry the dishes.

"Can I ask you something?" he asked suddenly.

Mia nodded putting the plates away. She hoisted herself up onto the counter and waited for him to speak.

"Why do you hate me so much?" he asked.

She opened her mouth in surprise. "You could tell?"

"I have eyes."

"Do you really?" she asked with a snort.

"Sure, I may have implied you were a waiting prostitute but it was a dimly lit balcony and all I saw was your chest. But that wasn't the only reason you hated me."

When she raised an eyebrow at that, he added, "It was a mighty fine chest, by the way. Very, um, sturdy."

Mia's eyes shone with mirth. "Sturdy, huh? I wonder how many women you must've insulted in your life for you to now be able to tell just by looking that they have more than one reason to hate you."

"Well," he leaned in conspiratorially. "Two. I called Leah a little girl, and asked to see her mother the day I met her."

"What?" Mia choked.

Westley made to get up to somehow help her but she waved him off. "You're a lucky man, living this long after that."

"Lehman saved me. Made it seem like it was a joke. Leah eyed me with murder for two months straight but I eventually won her over and we've been good friends ever since."

"How'd you manage that?" Mia asked, curious.

"I added her to my will."

"Wow, you're an idiot."

"Yeah…"

"You *bought* her forgiveness," she giggled.

"Trust me when I say it wasn't cheap and I really needed it," he laughed.

Mia snorted. "I bet."

"So… why do you hate me?"

Mia blinked, wondering if it was worth the trouble, and then shrugged. "Screw it. Do you remember the Gateway company merger that would have never been?"

Westley grinned. "I do. My friend's ex-wife was a battle-axe."

"I represented that battle-axe and during my presentation, you interrupted and shut down everything I had put together. Months of research and numbers, blown over by a pretty boy saying, 'We have no proof any of that could work'."

75

Westley gaped. "That… that was you?"

She nodded, the bitterness creeping back in.

"Oh. Well." Westley looked down at his glass. "I have a confession to make. Deciding against that deal was a petty thing, not a business decision. It was true it hadn't been done and the numbers all made sense but honestly, he just wanted to hurt his ex and, I was an asshole then and did what I thought was necessary."

"You threw me off with your interruptions," she accused. "Everything I had practiced over and over just left my head. I was so nervous and I couldn't recover myself in time." She remembered how she'd stuttered and finally, had her senior partner take over before it got awkward for everyone else. It had already been awkward for her.

"I did think you were a little green," he said softly "But by all rights, you should have won. Why didn't May say anything? "

May was the senior partner, Mia' boss. She wasn't surprised Westley was on a first name basis with her.

Mia frowned. "She said she wanted me to win on my own and I wouldn't get my confidence back if she stepped in then before I'd let her."

"She did fix it all some weeks later. With the very same proposal."

Mia nodded. "I know but... I'd still lost *my* chance."

Westley met her eye when she looked up. "I'm sorry about that."

Mia rolled her eyes. "You didn't even remember me."

"I remembered you as the hot angry woman who glared daggers at me. I'm sure I would have remembered your hate-filled glare more clearly had the lights been on. You left before the meeting was done."

Her eyes glimmered with humour. "I was worried I was going to throw a laptop at you."

Westley laughed. "I would definitely have remembered you then."

Mia considered throwing a knife at him but decided she was too young to go to jail for his murder.

They sat in silence for a minute before she got to her feet and stretched.

"Thank you for lunch. Remember, if you ever make too much food..."

"I know where to find you."

77

"Right at the kitchen door," she said with a laugh.

Mia waved as she left and completely missed the way Westley's eyes roamed her body as she did.

-

Recipe for Understanding

- 2 tablespoon sugar
- ¼ cup water
- 3 tablespoon cocoa
- 1 cup hot milk
- ¼ teaspoon vanilla essence
- Marshmallows

- ➤ Dissolve sugar in hot water till almost unbearably sweet. Frown.
- ➤ Add cocoa. Mix until thick. Breathe in. Consider making brownies instead.
- ➤ Add milk. Heat but do not boil. If milk starts to boil, give it a stern talking to.
- ➤ Add vanilla essence.
- ➤ Stir.
- ➤ Add marshmallows.
- ➤ Drink.

Note: Best served on cold days. If cold days unavailable, turn on air conditioning and proceed with recipe.

Chapter 4: Recipe for Understanding

-

The weekend passed with them greeting each other as they passed and Westley made lunch and dinner on Sunday after Mia found a place that *did* deliver to their house on Saturday night.

They'd watched TV while they ate and actually talked about annoying people they had at their workplaces that they found more irritating than they did each other.

During the week, Westley cooked dinner and Mia stayed in the kitchen as he did, helping where she could and cleaning up after him.

It was an odd pattern they created but it was manageable and after each meal, they returned to their rooms to work, saying variations of goodnight that were wishes of doom at best.

"Bed bugs."

"Night mares."

Their truce was in effect after all.

After a week of pleasantness however, Westley found that it wasn't meant to last.

He'd started on lunch but Mia hadn't left her room.

He assumed she had had a late night and needed to sleep in but long after he was done and the scent of curry chicken was wafting through the house, she still didn't come out.

Westley walked to Mia's door and knocked.

He wondered if he would have heard her leave her room if she left quietly.

He knocked again and when no answer came, he slowly pushed open the door, and almost heaved a sigh of relief when he saw her comforters molding her in the shape of the comforting foetal position. That meant Mia was around.

She was just in bed.

Possibly down with the periods, Westley thought to himself and imagined Leah smacking him for implying menstruation was like a cold.

He had never been in her room. She'd at least drawn back her heavy curtains and the light shining through the sheer drapes poured in easily.

Greens and blues decorated her room, a pale blue lamp, a simple painting of a forest, green carpeting, and blue furniture.

He wondered if she'd chosen the room as it was or brought stuff in.

It was warm and calming.

And it smelled just like her- like green apples and vanilla.

Slowly, he walked towards the bed, stopping to stand beside his roommate.

Westley closed the door quietly and wondered if she'd heard him. She hadn't moved. He stared at the bed closely, a moment of panic hitting him before he saw movement.

The pile of beddings shook and let out a sob. Westley started.

"Mia?"

She made a soft sound but didn't answer. "Hey," he said softly, walking slowly toward her bed.

"Hey," he said again in a low voice.

She didn't say anything and he frowned. If something bad had happened to her, maybe he should call Leah. Maybe she already had. Maybe this wasn't his place…

He stopped. He was chickening out when she was possibly hurt or in pain.

Maybe they weren't the best of friends but there was no way he was just going to leave her alone without knowing if she needed him, or needed *someone* and would settle for him.

"Are you alright?" he asked, gently touching what he hoped was her shoulder. When she shrugged him off without displacing her sheets from around her, he figured it definitely was her shoulder.

"I need you to not take this the wrong way," Mia's voice was thick and monotonous. She had obviously been crying. "But please go away."

Westley sighed.

She had to leave sometime.

She apparently didn't seem to think so.

Westley placed her plate of food on the table and left her room. When he went back hours later, neither the food nor the woman had moved.

He cleared the food away and brought her fresh food. Some of it had been eaten and he noticed her towel thrown haphazardly in her laundry basket.

At least she was bathing.

"Do you want me to call Leah?" he asked.

"No," she muttered and he left a plate of food and left again.

That went on for the rest of the day and the next day was Monday. He wondered if she would bother going in for work given how she was acting. He was worried but she didn't seem to be trying to hurt herself. He'd snuck in while she was asleep and raided her medicine cabinet. If she'd noticed, she hadn't said anything.

The next day, Westley told her he'd put some leftovers in the fridge and was leaving. It was awkward but he wasn't comfortable leaving her alone.

Mia didn't get up to get ready for work, and Westley didn't make her. He barely focused on his own projects that morning.

He looked at his copy of the lease and gave in after a moment, taking Mia's number and dialling.

She didn't pick up.

Westley left hurriedly telling his secretary he had a lunch meeting somewhere and to cancel the rest of his day. When he got back home, he was relieved to find the pile of blankets still breathing even if the woman hadn't moved.

By dinnertime, Westley was getting more than a little worried. Granted, he hadn't been there the whole day so Mia may have gotten up to eat or use the bathroom but whatever was bothering her, he didn't know what to do. He'd respected her decision to not call Leah but he was going to disrespect that soon enough.

Westley padded towards her bed and gently shook her shoulder. "Mia?"

"Go away," she muttered from beneath the blankets. Westley sighed.

"I won't go away. Not until you tell me what's going on."

He moved away from Mia's bed and sat at her desk. He'd replaced the leftovers and thrown out the food she'd left to be eaten by invisible starving faeries.

"What for?" came the muffled reply.

Westley sighed. "You're not eating, not moving and you're starting to smell."

The last one wasn't true but he was trying to get a rise out of her.

"If I smell so bad, why don't you get out?"

Westley scowled at that.

She sounded so defeated, so broken and hopeless and it made him angry.

Westley stormed towards the bed and grabbed the blankets. He yanked them off of her and threw them to the floor.

"What the hell are you doing?!" Mia yelled, springing out of her foetal position to face Westley. He was sure he heard some bones crack but didn't think it was the time to mock her.

Mia was wearing nothing but a tank top and short shorts and her hair was wild about her. Brown eyes blazed with offended fury and her lower lip wobbled slightly. Westley had to stop himself from admiring his housemate's body.

"If you won't tell me what's wrong, at least get up and eat," Westley ordered, narrowing his eyes, daring her to disobey.

"Screw you," Mia spat, turning her back on Westley and lying back down. She had no intention of going anywhere.

Westley had had enough.

He grabbed her beddings and left the room with them. He returned with three nerf guns. He'd debated using them instead of paintball guns and had simply put them away after George told them off.

But this wasn't a prank. It was a necessary evil.

He threw one on the bed and when Mia looked up to ask him what he thought he was doing, he shot her leg.

"What the hell is your problem?!" Mia demanded angrily, grabbing at her leg. The foam darts stung but wouldn't do any serious damage. He had two guns with him and had only graced her with one.

"Right now, you are."

"Look. We're not friends. And we were doing just *fine* ignoring each other. How about you get back to it and *leave me alone*!" Mia turned to return to her position, but Westley didn't let her.

He shot her again, once.

From the way she froze, her only flinch having been when the dart hit her skin, he knew he shouldn't have. He knew that.

That was the last straw for Mia, and she spun around, grabbing the gun and shooting him twice on the forehead.

"You could have shot me in the eye," Westley accused, rubbing at his forehead. Mia said nothing. She shot him and kept shooting him. Westley turned away from her and cursed until he heard the click.

She was out of bullets.

Westley turned but found that she'd moved and grabbed his gun from his loose grip.

Westley tried to duck as best he could but she was standing in a way that implied she didn't care if he shot her or where he hit her.

He took his other gun and aimed. He missed a lot and it seemed Mia was a lot more careful with the second gun's bullets. She wasn't missing and she was taking her time. In the end, however, Westley was victorious. He charged the tiny distance at her as she aimed and he jumped onto her, tackling her. In seconds he was straddling her stomach and had her arms pinned above her head.

"Now that *that's* over," Westley said with a wide grin, his body still stinging from all the darts that had struck him, "Would you like to tell me *what* the *hell* is going on with you?"

Mia struggled under him, trying to buck him off of her, her hair splayed. Westley pushed away the thought of how beautiful she looked like that, with murder in her eyes and everything.

"I told you to leave me alone!" she shouted.

"And I clearly ignored you," he said calmly, as if he could do that all day.

"What do you want from me?" she said, still struggling but weaker.

"Must I repeat myself constantly?"

"Go to hell."

"I guess you don't mind being like this till you tell me. I can fall asleep sitting upright, by the way," he said. "It's pretty easy."

Mia's chest was rising and falling quickly, her breathing heavy from her attempt to get out from under him. He was leaning over her to keep an easy hold on her wrists and their eyes held for long moments. He took the chance to study her.

There were bags under her eyes and they were puffy from all her crying. But she was still fierce. Even with the wet lashes and snot.

When Westley didn't say anything else, Mia shut her eyes tightly.

"Please…"

Westley didn't let go.

She sniffed and he leaned in, waiting.

"My boyfriend just told me he's seeing someone else," Mia said.

Westley blinked in confusion. "I thought you broke up."

Mia laughed bitterly and opened her eyes. Tears slid to her ears. "We did. Well, we were on a break. He always…"

She made a helpless sound and Westley finished the sentence for her.

"He always does this."

Westley stared at Mia, not quite sure what to say to that. He saw more tears welling in her eyes and she squeezed them shut again.

"*Dammit,*" she whispered, tears spilling from beneath her clenched eyelids.

Westley hesitated and then slowly released her hands and sat up, still straddling her.

"I don't know what to say…" he trailed off.

He felt like an absolute cad. He'd obviously forced her to reveal something she hadn't wanted to reveal. His intentions had been good but he wasn't quite sure about the execution. "Mia, I—"

He was cut off as Mia shoved him roughly off of her. He lost his balance and fell off of the bed. He was lucky her carpet was thick.

"I don't want your sympathy," she said venomously. "Get out."

She turned around and marched to her door. She threw open the door, and motioned for him to use it.

Westley walked to the door and stepped close to her. She looked up defiantly at him, furious brown meeting amused blue.

He gave her a cheeky grin. "Oh look, you're out of bed."

She was tempted to strangle him but settled for attempting to make her door hit his ass on his way out.

-

Recipe for Friendship

- 5 large lasagne sheets
- ½ kg mincemeat
- ½ medium onion, diced
- 3 garlic cloves, diced
- 3 large tomatoes, grated
- 1 can tomato paste
- ½ teaspoon black pepper
- 2 cups water
- 2 large eggs
- 4 cups mozzarella cheese, shredded

➤ Soak lasagne sheets for five to ten minutes in hot water. Drain.
➤ Cook mincemeat for 10 minutes with oil of choice, onions and garlic, in a large pan (non-stick, like your last relationship).
➤ Stir in the tomatoes and paste, water, herbs and spices of choice including black pepper and salt. Boil. Reduce heat. Simmer (like you during arguments in your last relationship).
➤ In separate bowl, mix eggs, cheese and salt.
➤ Preheat oven to 190 degrees Celsius.
➤ Put meat sauce in square baking dish. Layer with pre-soaked lasagne sheets. Then egg and cheese mixture. Then meat and sauce. Repeat.
➤ Fill dish. Top with meat sauce, meat and cheese.
➤ Bake for 20 to 25 minutes covered. Uncover and bake 20 minutes or until bubbly.

Note: With friendship and lasagne, one must always pay attention (to the oven temperature) and listen well (to the timer going off). To truly test the strength of one's friendship, burn the lasagne and serve it anyway.

Chapter 5: Recipe for Friendship

-

When Westley got to Leah's house, she came out looking ready to scold him.

Leah was wearing a shirt that was obviously from George as it had his ironclad "*Refund* means nothing to me unless you mean you're paying me again" mantra printed on it.

"Westley. Wha—"

"I don't want Mia to break the lease," he said abruptly.

Leah looked at him, at his car in her driveway and at the streetlights that had just come on.

"You couldn't have texted this to me?" she asked. "What happened?"

He didn't exactly know why he'd driven the whole way to complain about the stubborn woman he'd left in his new home but it had seemed like the right thing to do. He had heard her slam the door and go into the kitchen and he had hightailed it like a wise man. She was angry and aware of where the knives were. Nothing good could come from that.

But there was also something else. The woman had grown on him a little.

Their tenuous friendship was one he enjoyed.

If he was being completely honest with himself, Mia reminded him of Gigi.

But he felt protective of her, even though they still weren't technically friends.

Leah said slowly. "Well?"

Westley was silent for a moment. "Mia's ex texted her and said he's seeing someone. She's been locked up in her room for days. I didn't know whether to call you or not because she asked me not to but I was really worried about her so I went in there today and shot her. But then-"

"You *shot* her?" Leah asked, her voice dangerously low.

"With a nerf gun!" he clarified quickly. She had looked like she was about to do some shooting of her own.

"Anyway, I couldn't think of any other way to get her out of her blanketed cocoon so... I think I just pissed her off. Especially 'cause she told me about it."

Leah watched Westley carefully as he spoke. He seemed genuinely concerned for Mia.

"She said he does this all the time."

Leah sighed and nodded. "Come in."

Westley followed her to her kitchen and saw Lehman there. The man nodded at him and left the room when he got a look from his wife.

"You're kind of scary," Westley said after seeing that.

She shrugged. "Sit."

He sat at her kitchen table and she put the kettle on.

She bustled around the kitchen, putting biscuits and other tiny baked treats on a plate and placing that in front of him.

"I knew something like that had happened," Leah said. "Mia's been texting me and not mentioning anything about Eric."

Westley frowned at that but Leah gave him a sad smile. "She doesn't want to hear me say 'I told you so' even though she knows I wouldn't do that. She also doesn't want me to pity her or comfort her. She's done this before. Sometimes I go get her out of it. This time... I wanted to see if she could do it herself."

"What do you mean?"

"Mia was very sheltered growing up. Her parents are wonderful people but they wanted to protect their only child from the world. She didn't have go on dates or hang out with boys. The first boy she met who showed her even the smallest bit of interest, she attached herself to like a barnacle."

"Eric?"

"Eric," she nodded. "She put all the romantic expectations she'd imagined for herself onto him. He was witty and smart and non-conforming. He was studying philosophy at the time, before he switched to something else as he was wont to do. She was studying law and felt that whole opposites attract thing. Eric was her soul mate and she wouldn't hear any different."

Westley thanked her when she handed him the hot cup of tea and continued. "At this point I'm not sure if she loves him or if she's just wasted so much time that she can't see it not working out."

"But he's told her he's seeing someone else."

Leah snorted. "He's probably been sleeping with someone else for a long time and just now thought to mention it."

"I don't get why they stay in touch."

"He manipulates her. He's emotionally abusive and she just takes it all. They've been broken up but he always keeps in touch when he feels like it, just to remind her that he still exists in case she forgets. She gets hopeful from those 'just checking up on you', 'hey I missed you', 'I was wrong' messages. Usually at that point, he's slept with and grown bored of his new conquest or his time as the starving artist with a new muse is starting to wear thin."

"He mooches off of her?"

"Not really. He has family money. He just enjoys having her around.
"

"How do you know?"

"He once told me that he'll marry her. That regardless of how much I hate him, he could have her just like *that*," she snapped her fingers.

Westley's expression darkened at that. "Did you tell her what he said?"

Leah raised an eyebrow at him. "Tell the woman who is sobbing over her ex and not at all thinking he's an ass after what he did? Would she believe me? I got her out of the house to deal with her feelings. I checked their apartment and he moved back in. With his new girlfriend."

"You didn't tell her."

"She would only go there and cause a scene. Maybe burn the place down or something."

He thought of the proud beautiful, spitfire, who was also a lawyer, with her violent tendencies and supposed it was a valid fear. Though she'd likely plead insanity.

Leah smiled wistfully. "Love makes people stupid but with Mia, it's like she loses all but two brain cells."

"Can I ask you something?" Westley asked after burning his tongue on her tea.

Leah nodded for him to go ahead.

"Why are you telling me all this?"

Leah looked at him, her hands wrapped around her teacup. "Because you care about her. You wouldn't have been an annoying ass just to get her out of bed for the fun of it."

"I really would, actually," he said.

Leah rolled her eyes at him. "You two are clearly too volatile to even live together but I do think you'd be good friends and with how things seem to have been going, without getting blood on the beautiful tiles George had installed, I'm sure you could be the best of friends."

"You're only saying that because there's something in it for you," Westley accused.

Leah grinned. "Well, of course. "

"So, how do I... fix her?" Westley asked after a long moment.

"She's not one of your projects, Westley. You can't throw money and focus groups at her until she gets fixed."

Westley snorted. "I wouldn't throw *focus groups* at her..."

"Please, don't throw money at my friend." Leah said. "Just... be there for her. Now finish your tea and get out of my house. You're wasting all my good air."

Westley burned the rest of his mouth and stood up, leaving the house. Lehman came in after and made himself a cup, joining his wife at the table. "Mia will be angry you told him that."

Leah shrugged. "I can take her."

Lehman chuckled, "Look at Westley though, finally caring about someone other than himself."

Leah smiled and slid a slice of cake to her husband. "They have so much in common they don't even realise it."

***

When Westley got back, loud music was playing and Mia was in the living room in baggy overalls- painting the walls.

He gaped. "What the…"

She looked back at him and smiled widely, her eyes bright. He was caught off guard by the look of careless joy she gave him- like she was pleased to see him.

That was when he noticed the bottles on the ground.

She was drunk.

She was painting their living room. And drunk.

For a drunk person attempting DIY painting, she'd had enough sense to at least move the furniture away.

Westley grimaced when he thought of the future homelessness George would impose on them but then he took in a deep breath and calmed down.

George hadn't forbidden it…

"Come help!" Mia called, offering a brush.

There was paint on her face and she had opened seven cans. He wondered where she'd gotten them.

"Where'd you buy the paint?"

"I found it in the garage. Pretty colours," she said, nodding seriously at her haphazard work.

The white walls of the living room were now streaked with yellow and green and splatterings of orange and blue.

It looked terrible.

"What are you doing?"

"Painting," she said like it was a matter of fact. "Obviously. Are you blind?"

"Okay, painting. Why?" he approached her slow like one would a wild animal.

"I wanted to apologize for earlier," she said. "I know you were only being an asshole to be helpful."

"Hey, don't worry about it but um… Why did you decide to paint the living room as an apology?"

She grinned and she looked so much like a child that Westley laughed despite himself.

"You seem to like games. Shooting and stuff. So I'm making a game room and we can have the target practice on this wall…"

.She hiccoughed and dropped the brush and looked at it like she was surprised it had succumbed to gravity.

Westley sighed.

She turned to him with a small frown. "My brush dropped."

Westley laughed and picked it up for her.

When she was sober, he would apologize for shooting her earlier.

He went to the kitchen and came back with a wet cloth.

She was standing in the same position staring at the brush and

"You're a mess," he said and reached out to take Mia's chin in his hand. Mia jerked away with a glare, but Westley only sighed and grabbed her again. "Hold still. You're still cute, just a bit too… splattered."

"I - huh?"

"Hold still," Westley said softly.

The light brown eyes widened, but Mia didn't move away. Westley ignored the soft feel of her skin, focusing intently on wiping off the green and orange specks from her cheek. It all seemed to be water paint. It came off a lot easier than he had thought it would.

There was a bit of blue on her lower tip and Westley brushed it off easily with his finger and then froze. Her lips were full, wet and soft. They'd parted slightly when he'd touched her and he couldn't look away.

"Am I all clean now?" she asked and Westley realised he'd been staring. He dropped his hand like she burned him.

"All clean."

"I want some juice," she said suddenly.

"It's in the kitchen," he replied dryly.

"Carry me."

He snorted. "Like hell."

"Okay," she pouted and then made like she was walking to the kitchen only to jump on his back once he moved out of her way to give her room to pass.

"What the hell!" he yelled, barely catching his balance and gripping her thighs and leaning forward quickly to keep her from falling off of him and cracking her head open on the tiles.

"To the kitchen!" she laughed.

He considered dropping her and she seemed to sense it because she tightened her arms around him immediately.

He felt her breasts press against his back through her rough clothing and he prayed for calm.

"Fine," he muttered and shifted her, almost dropping her when she spread her arms in glee. "Dammit! No more dessert for you!"

"*Are you calling me fat?*"

"Just... hold on and... please, be quiet."

Mia glared, even though Westley couldn't see her. He made his way to the kitchen slowly and plopped her onto the bar stool.

He handed her a glass of juice and she drank it quickly.

"Why were you drinking?" he asked.

She shrugged.

He sighed. "Come on, I'll help you finish George's lawsuit against us."

"What?"

"The living room wall."

She grinned. "Really?"

He nodded and she jumped off the stool. "Okay!"

She dragged him and they went back to the living room.

Westley took off his shirt and grabbed a brush. Mia sang along to her playlist, dancing and occasionally pulling him along to dance with her.

He smiled

They painted for hours. They talked about growing up, about their parents, about the joys of being only-children… and by the time he realised it, it was dawn.

He noticed Mia slowly sobering up but she kept painting and he went right along with it.

They drew their curtains back and let the sun shine on the wall they'd painted.

It looked like something raw sewage would bubble up.

Westley quickly called the professionals while Mia checked their lease for whether there was something about painting and being sued.

Hours later, the two sat side-by-side on the couch, tiredly watching the professionals fix everything they'd ruined.

They shut the door behind the last guy and laughed to themselves at the lecture they'd been given about how DIYing was a pointless industry trying to take money from good folks like them who'd only mess up and call professionals like they should have in the first place.

"Sleepy?" Mia asked in a low voice.

Wes nodded. "Mm. Sleepy."

"Hey," her voice was now barely above a whisper and she sounded exhausted. "Thanks for shooting me earlier."

Westley smiled and turned when he felt a weight on his shoulder.

She had fallen asleep by his side.

-

Recipe for Beginnings

- Purchase a book on Banting
- Low carb, high fat (moderate hell yes)
- Eat only when hungry
- Curb your alcohol intake (Pardon?)

- ➤ Trip to the grocery store
- ➤ Spend much money
- ➤ So worth it

Note:

- New Year, New You.
- Mind Over Matter.
- You'll Eat When You're Dead (Realise you may not have thought this through).

Chapter 6: Recipe for Beginnings

-

Leah hosted another event and this time didn't even have to threaten the both of them or invite one while the other's fairy godmother was stuck in traffic.

They were both present at the charity ball and Leah had told them that the only reason she'd invited them was because Max had made a bet with her.

She hadn't divulged the terms of the bet and had simply said they should both show up cause, "Momma has some bucks to win".

Westley offered to drive and had patiently, yelling every five minutes, waited for Mia to finish getting ready.

He had shut up when she'd come out threatening bodily harm with the sharp ends of her purse but that wasn't what had shut him up.

Her dark blue dress clung to her curves in all the right places, showing off her full figure. The slit went up to the middle of her thigh and her chest hinted at cleavage, fully covered and going over one shoulder. Her hair was up in a messy bun with loose curls falling freely where they wanted. She turned, letting him see her from every angle and making him imagine-

"What do you think?" she asked, interrupting his less than decent thoughts.

Her eyes-

Gosh, her eyes.

Westley cleared his throat. "Yes, very nice."

She snorted. "*Nice*? I look *amazing*, don't I?"

"Yes and you left your humility in your other purse."

"Hey!" She smacked him with her purse and he laughed, tugging her closer.

She chuckled and he smiled down at her, blue eyes softening as he held her. "You look wonderful."

Her cheeks tinged with pink and she smiled almost shyly, pleased at his compliment. "Thanks, your turn for the once over."

"Do I have to?"

"Turn," she made the gesture with a finger, showing him he should twirl.

He grudgingly did and she wolf whistled.

"Don't treat me like a piece of meat."

"Not even prime rib?"

"Stop objectifying me."

"Moron," she laughed. "Come on, let's go. You've delayed us enough as it is."

Westley gaped at her audacity.

She chuckled and waited while he locked up.

They decided to entertain themselves by playing twenty-one questions the whole evening; if at all Leah would let them run free of course.

"If you can't answer a question, you have to take a shot," she declared.

"Slow down there Alcoholic Annie, I'm not carrying you back here. You can't answer, you take a sip of a disgusting cocktail."

She sighed. "Fine, grandma."

They made the rounds when they got there, greeting Leah and Lehmann and letting them meet other people and show them off around the room-

"*The* Westley Nott, of Notta Diamonds yes-"

"-Miss Rhodes, record for highest marks in the bar, partner at May, June and Jones. You represented my company last year. That was great work. I hear you made partner-"

When Leah gave them some reprieve, Westley groaned. "I feel like a show pony. She crooks a finger at us and we go and she acts like a parent telling their relatives how their kindergartner is just so darn special."

Mia smiled at the description. It fit perfectly.

Westley got them their gross cocktails, the 'Kopala tumble' and leaned back against the counter. "Spit or swallow?" he asked.

Mia smiled mischievously at him. "*Bite.*"

"Mm," he said. "And *then* do you swallow?"

Mia threw the cocktail umbrella at him.

"Your aim was better the first time," he said with a laugh after he caught it easily.

She made a face at him and asked, "What is it exactly that you *do*?"

He grinned and sipped from his cocktail. She gave him a dry look.

"Do you watch porn?" he asked with a mischievous look.

"For the comment section only," she replied with a sly grin. "It's comedy gold. And sometimes, very uplifting and supportive."

116

"Uh huh."

"Scout's honour."

"You were never a scout."

"Doesn't make me any less honourable."

"Actually-"

"Next question," she said, elbowing him as they walked slowly through the room. They stopped to greet the CEO of the Zambian A to Z branch and moved on. Leah had been very strict about them mingling and 'working the room'.

"First pet?" he asked.

"A rabbit."

"Seriously?"

"He vanished mysteriously after he escaped from his cage and my mom found his poop pellets all over the living room carpet," she explained. "First apartment?"

"Someplace unpleasant," he said.

"Really?"

"My parents didn't want me to be spoiled. I had to start from the bottom."

"I would have thought you had a nice little place with a view in Roma," Mia said.

"I do now." Wes shrugged. "Well, *did*. My ex-girlfriend decided I needed some space before things got more serious. She suggested I move out and figure out what it is I want. I sold it because, well, memories."

"Was it that supermodel…Gigi?"

"Not your turn to ask," he smirked. "First boyfriend?"

"Eric," she answered grudgingly.

"Seriously?"

Instead of confirming, she turned and said, "Not your turn to ask. Is Gigi the ex you mean?"

He made a face and nodded. "Yes, her. It was in all the papers."

She shrugged. "I get all my news from forwarded messages from my parents. Mostly apocalyptic stuff and how some single woman choked on a samosa and died without leaving her parents any grandkids."

"Tragic stuff," Westley said somberly.

"Truly."

"Do you still want to get back with your ex?" he asked.

"I think so. Don't you still want yours?" she countered.

"I think so."

Mia rolled her eyes. "Men."

"What? You gave the exact same answer!"

"The circumstances are completely different," she huffed. "Mine is a lying douchebag and yours seems to just want you to be sure you want to be with her."

"You could tell all that from the couple of sentences I just said?"

"I'm wildly perceptive," she replied. "Anyway, why can't it be a simple 'Yes, I want her and only her'? Why can't you ever be sure of yourselves?"

Wes shrugged, knowing she was asking partly about Eric. "It's a huge decision. You need to think about it to be sure."

"I like to think that when the right person comes along, you won't waste time thinking because they could slip away while you're there pondering."

"It's not that simple," he said.

She snorted. "It really is. If you keep finding excuses not to be with someone, you shouldn't be with them."

"How do you figure that?"

"You don't throw away what you don't want to leave."

Westley watched her for a moment before he put their glasses on the tray of a passing waiter and grabbed two glasses of wine.

Mia took the offered glass and he nudged her gently with his elbow as they turned to watch the crowd.

"So why did you move out from your apartment?" he asked.

"Too many memories," Mia said.

"Ex memories?"

She shrugged noncommittally, taking a sip of her drink instead of answering, even though it wasn't his turn.

She was about to ask him a question when someone threw an arm around her. She turned to find Max grinning at them, obviously well on his way to being quite drunk.

"I got bored watching you two be civil to each other," Max complained. He was dressed in a slim fit suit and his hair was cut neatly and like always, his face was as clean-shaven as a baby's bottom, his light brown skin glowing.

"Glitter in your lotion?" Mia asked, peering closely at his flawless skin.

"Don't insult me, peasant," he said with a scoff. "My skin's just perfect."

"How long have you been here?" Westley asked, "We didn't see you when we were 'working the room'."

"Oh, I was upstairs looking down on the masses and judging them accordingly," Max said dismissively. "But everyone is being so prim and proper. It's been quite a letdown."

"This is a charity event," Mia laughed.

"Yes, yes, save the children and the world, but would you look at Leah over there, flirting with her own husband," Max said with a grimace.

"Yes, it's quite sickening, isn't it?" Westley said with a nod.

"I think they might even go home later and have marital sex with each other," Mia added.

"When will the madness end?" Max whispered before he saw Leah walking up to them.

"I hope everyone is behaving," Leah said.

"Yes ma'am," the three replied.

"Good," she said, amused. "Oh hey, Westley, I was hoping to have you meet one more pair of guests."

Westley blinked. "Oh? Who?"

When her smile turned evil, he put his glass in Max's hands and made for the door.

Unfortunately, he came face to face with the very people he was trying to preemptively escape from.

"Westley!"

Westley had all of three seconds before the fifty year old woman was attached to his side with the grip of a barnacle.

He sighed in her embrace, "Mom, hey."

He glared at Leah who simple smiled and waved as she walked away.

Mia tried to do the same, not exactly sure why, but found her hand in someone else's. "Hello, there."

She smiled awkwardly at the handsome older man who was shaking her hand. "Hello."

"I'm Westley's father, William," he said pleasantly. "The woman cutting off his oxygen is my wife, Sammie. Who are you?"

"Mia," she said, noting that Max had somehow vanished. The bastard. "Mia Rhodes."

"Lovely to meet you," the man said, his blue eyes crinkling. Westley had inherited his father's eyes.

The woman finally let go of Westley and turned to Mia. She was really beautiful, ageing but definitely ageing well. Her hair was just starting to gray and several strands were matching her gray eyes.

Sammie Nott opened her arms and pulled Mia into a hug. "So nice to meet you, dear," she said before turning to her husband. "Who is she?"

"Mia Rhodes," he provided.

"Ah yes, Mia, lovely name. Nice to meet you."

"Nice to meet you too," Mia said with a smile.

"Why are you here?" Westley asked his parents. "Not that I'm not glad to see you,"

"We were in the neighborhood."

"You live several provinces away. And this is a charity ball."

"Well, being wealthy and all, we can afford to donate some money," William said in amusement. "Besides, we're your parents and we were getting worried about you. You rarely communicate. We had to make sure you were alright."

"We communicate *every day* in misunderstood memes and shaky video calls," he protested. "And you never mentioned that you were coming."

They both ignored him and turned to Mia. "What about your family? Where are they from?"

"They live in Lusaka West," She said. "Over an hour's drive from here. We too communicate in memes and shaky video calls."

"See them often?"

"We meet mostly at weddings and funerals."

"Sort of like us," William said, looking pointedly at his son.

"Excuse us for a moment," Westley said, tugging Mia's hand and leading her away from his parents. He walked to the nearby window sitting near a large cactus plant and when they both turned back, his parents waved.

"Your parents are awesome," she laughed.

"And embarrassing."

"Yes. That's what I said. Awesome."

"Please help me out," he whispered when he saw his parents coming over to them.

"Why? I hate you," she grinned.

"Yes, I know," Westley replied equably. "I feel the same way about you."

"But," she added, touching his arm gently. "I don't want you to die a horrible death anymore."

"You're too generous."

"Maybe a nice quiet death. In your sleep."

"Just like my good ol' grandma," he said.

"I'm sorry," she looked concerned. "Were you close?"

"She's still alive but we keep our fingers crossed."

"What a horrible thing to say."

"You've never met her. It's probably the nicest thing anyone has ever said about her," Westley replied.

"They're almost here, what do you want me to do?" Mia asked as she saw his parents approaching.

Westley thought quickly. "Just… try not to say anything. Smile and look pretty."

Mia raised an eyebrow at that but didn't speak as Mr. and Mrs. Nott joined them.

"Were you trying to escape us?" Mrs. Nott asked.

"Advice was given to smile and say nothing," Mia replied with a smile and Westley gave her a murderous glare.

"You're not one for advice are you?" Mr. Nott said with a chuckle.

"I just assumed it was given to Gerald."

"Gerald?"

"The plant," she said, pointing at the cactus. "And I'll be damned if he isn't doing a splendid job of it."

Sammie laughed. "So how long have you two been dating?"

"Oh no, we aren't dating," Mia said, looking over at Westley who seemed just as surprised as her.

"What makes you think we're dating?" he asked his parents.

"You suddenly moved in with a woman after being unable to stick with one for longer than a night," his dad replied easily. "Leah says you're quite happy now."

Westley and Mia both gaped and then turned to look at Leah who was watching them and were amazed when she smiled sweetly and made shooing gestures at them. She'd spun his parents quite the tale.

Westley turned back to his parents. "Leah must be...mistaken. And what do you mean *'unable to stick with one for longer than a night'*? I dated Gertrude for three years."

His parents stared at him.

"Wait? *Seriously*?" Sammie asked.

"Yes," he deadpanned.

"But... her name was *Gertrude*," William said in confusion and his wife nodded as if that was a perfectly valid point.

"...and?" Westley asked.

"I mean… Did you find her in an old age home?" Sammie asked, waving a waiter away when he offered her a drink.

"Mom-"

"Could you even say her name in bed with a straight face?" his father asked.

Mia almost choked on the drink she'd been sipping and then she paused. "Wait a minute… Gigi's real name…is Gertrude?"

When his parents nodded and Westley groaned, Mia gave a polite cough and excused herself.

"Don't you *dare* tell Max," Westley hissed.

Mia muttered to herself and moved back to his side.

She spent the next few minutes listening to Westley assure his parents that he had indeed been dating the supermodel-whose-name-was-really-Gertrude. After promising to call more and visit more and eat more, his parents finally left him alone.

"So," Mia said as they walked away. "… Gertrude."

"Don't."

"What?" she nudged him with her elbow. "We talked about *my* ex."

"I didn't ask you to," he answered gruffly.

She grinned, unperturbed. "You *will* tell me all about Gertrude."

Westley knew he'd regret ever mentioning Gertrude's name but he'd refused to call her Gigi once they'd started dating and she hadn't wanted him to.

His dad was right though.

He hadn't ever said her name in bed.

***

Westley drove them home as while Mia hadn't consumed too much, she wasn't the best at holding her liquor.

He had put her to bed, covering his eyes as she undressed and then covering her with a blanket when she'd yelled that she was cold. It had been amusing as hell.

And the next morning, he found her in their living room.

"You cannot handle your alcohol at all," Wes said with a laugh as he looked down at Mia who was lying face down on the carpeted floor and moaning about dying.

"Kill me," she whispered. "Make it quick."

"What are you doing in here?" he asked, sitting down next to her. He rubbed her hair absently and she was quiet for a moment before she said, "Eric sent me a text."

"What?"

She looked up abruptly. "He said he misses me and asked if we could meet."

Westley ignored the pang in his chest as he asked. "What did you say?"

She shook her head. "I didn't say anything. I'm not stupid. He's done this before."

"What do you want to do?" Westley asked.

She looked at him and then dropped back to the carpet and groaned at the movement. "I don't know. He's all I've ever known, you know. I don't know if I want him back because I'm used to him or..."

"Or?"

"Do I love him?" she asked Westley.

Westley patted her head gently. "I have no idea."

Mia sighed and then turned onto her back. She looked beautiful lying there and Westley wanted nothing more than to cover her body with his own and-

Whoa.

He shook his head and Mia said, "I have aspirin in my room if you need it."

He laughed, "Thanks but let's focus on you wanting to go back to your ex."

"Have you made us breakfast?" Mia asked instead and Westley snorted.

"Not yet, mistress."

"You should get started on that. I'll be here pondering."

"Or dying."

"Both," she said and then struggled up with his help. She stumbled and he caught her.

She was on her knees, her face close to his and she blinked. He noticed she was a bit unsteady and was speaking slower than usual.

"Would you believe Max asked me if something is going on between us?"

Westley wondered for a moment if he'd imagined her saying that. "Sorry, what?"

Her brown eyes bore into his blue and she looked amused.

"I've never been with anyone but Eric. He said it's good that I'm getting a new perspective other than missionary."

"And he thinks being on top of me is it?" he asked, not at all minding the view that came to mind.

"Or under," she said.

"Well that sounds boring," he said and didn't realize his voice had lowered to match hers. "Wait, you didn't tell him nothing was going on? Why does he think something is going on?"

"Something about how I easily gave up on *the plan*," she said. "And I haven't thrown you off of a balcony."

"Wow."

"Yeah. We haven't even been near a balcony in ages," she responded, pulling back to look at him.

Westley smiled in that infuriating way of his, cocking his head to the side. "Is that so?"

Mia nodded. "Yes. But I still hate you."

Westley laughed and patted her cheek. "Aw, I hate you, too."

"Now can we have breakfast?"

Westley chuckled. "Sure."

-

Recipe for Jealousy

> ➤ **See**: Recipe for Disaster

Chapter 7: Recipe for Jealousy

-

"Try this," Westley offered, absently holding out a chunk of his red velvet muffin for Mia to bite. She did, accidentally licking a stray bit of cream cheese that had lingered on Westlcy's fingers. Wes raised an eyebrow at that, warding off his own reaction, but Mia didn't seem to notice as she'd closed her eyes, enjoying his newest creation.

"I didn't know you could bake as well," she said with a sigh and a blissful expression. "I'm going to have to insist we increase your dowry. That's delicious."

"I thought you might like it," Westley said, his blue eyes bright with pride.

He sounded a tiny bit smug.

"I suppose I can be your taste taster," she said like she was going out of her way to help.

He snorted. "In that case, we'll need more ingredients. We're out of milk and eggs and… pretty much everything."

"I can go get them tomorrow if you give me a list," Mia said. "You make most of our meals so it's the least I could do."

"Let's go together *today*," he said, standing up.

"No can do," Mia said. "Today's wash day."

Wes blinked. "Pardon?"

"Wash day," she said slowly.
We shrugged, "Okay. well, we can use your car and stop by the car wash after-"

"Oh, *honey*," Mia covered her mouth to keep from giggling.

She pointed at her hair that was in chunky twists. "I'm washing my hair today."

He paused. "You select specific days to wash your hair?" he asked, amused.

"It's a taxing process," she replied.

"Fine," he said. "Wash it. I'll wait and-"

Mia laughed loud and long and hard.

"I need to do a protein treatment, then shampoo and deep condition and *then* air dry-"

"Why would you *air* dry? Just use a towel and-"

He stopped speaking when he saw her horrified look.

Mia got up quietly and went to her room to begin her wash day.

***

The next day, Wes was surly. He still didn't understand.

"I don't get why you need a whole day to wash your hair," he muttered. "Especially when it looks the same as it did yesterday."

Mia laughed and grabbed his hand, letting him hold some of her twists. Wes' eyes widened and he continued to squish and hair in his hands.

"It's so... soft and fluffy," he said in awe.

Mia looked smug. "Damn right it is."

He was an early riser and was already dressed for the day. Mia however, looked like a cute just-woke-up version of someone who had had no intention of ever waking up.

Westley knew that when he'd suggested grocery shopping together, he may come to regret it. Mia had come to show off her hair and then dashed off to get dressed for the outside world, changing into even baggier sweatpants and a t-shirt that said 'I'm with stupid' and an arrow pointing left. She walked out of the house pointedly walking on his right and insisting she'd drive so she would sit on his right, too. With her fluffy twists and baggy clothes, she had no right to look as beautiful as she did then.

Westley sighed as they entered the store. He was in jeans and a t-shirt and looked ready to face the sun while Mia was by his side, squinting at everything.

"Is there something wrong with your eyes?" he asked, raising an eyebrow at her.

"Everything is just *so bright*," she said. "I'm only here because you insisted I should find out where to buy things for you to cook for me."

"I do not recall ever saying that," he replied as they neared the vegetable section.

"I'm paraphrasing," she said.

"I don't trust you to buy any fresh produce," he said looking down at her, referring to the time he'd asked her to get a tomato from their garden and she had returned with an insult.

"That tomato was fresh," she smiled up at him.

"It was hard as a rock," he said drily.

"But still fresh."

"Go get some snacks or something," he sighed. "I'll handle the adult stuff."

"Yes, *mother*," she made a face at him and went off in search of snacks.

The store was huge and she found the snacks at the opposite end of it. The vegetables and whole foods were much closer to the exit and she marvelled at the punishment the store was obviously giving paying customers who just wanted some damn snacks.

She considered suing them as she made her way back to the vegetables, never once doubting that he would have taken anything less than twenty minutes inspecting a cabbage to the point of interrogating employees about its parentage and ivy league schooling.

When she got closer, she saw that he was indeed holding a cabbage in his hands but he wasn't looking at it.

Instead he was looking at a beautiful brunette who was beaming a bright smile at him.

Whatever he must have said to her must have really made her day.

Mia was surprised at the slight irritation she felt but she wondered if she should take some time to let him stand there flirting with a woman while holding a cabbage.

She decided she was being silly and should definitely not cockblock. Before she turned to go grab extra snacks, Westley's blue eyes found hers and his smile brightened.

She gave him a small awkward wave and walked over, tossing him his favourite packet of crisps when she was within reasonable throwing distance.

He caught it and threw it into the trolley. "Thanks."

The woman next to him looked slightly irritated at Mia's arrival but she smiled politely and offered her hand to Mia. "Hello, I'm Angela."

Mia blinked at the woman before dropping the rest of the snacks in the trolley and shaking her hand. "Mia, nice to meet you."

"I'm sorry," she said, eyes on Westley. "I didn't realise you were here with your girlfriend. I must seem quite rude."

Mia and Westley spoke at the same time. "Oh, we're not-"

Then they looked at each other and both rolled their eyes.

"We're not dating," Westley said, handing the cabbage over to Mia who assumed he'd deemed it suitable or ripe or something and put it in the trolley. "We live together. Uh, we're housemates."

The woman's look of ire reduced but only slightly. "Oh, I see," she laughed softly. "I'm sorry for assuming."

"Simple mistake," Mia said in a conspiratory tone. "Besides, I'm way out of his league."

Westley threw a packet of crisps at her and she caught it before noticing how the woman was watching them intently.

"I'll uh, go get some desserts and stuff," she announced, leaving them alone together. Westley had looked momentarily confused but nodded and waved.

When she got back, Angela was gone. She wriggled her eyebrows at him.

"Did you break your face?" he asked in amusement.

She laughed and said, "I saw you flirting. Was it good? Was it everything you dreamed it would be? Did you cum?"

"Good gosh woman, there are children nearby, have you no shame? And yes to all your questions."

Mia chuckled as they went through the aisles together this time.

"I got her number."

"Smooth," she teased. "And a date?"

They stopped in front of the magazine aisle and both of them found themselves staring at a huge blowout image of Gigi laughing at a restaurant with a man.

Mia turned to Westley slowly. "Are you alright?"

He shrugged. "I'm fine. It's not like she's cheating on me. We broke up ages ago."

Mia hummed and Westley gave her an irritated glance.

"Gigi is dating," Mia said. "And you're working late nights trying not to think about it. You should go out too. Just always be on time to make us dinner."

"You're a piece of work."

"Thanks," she said as they started walking again. "So, date?"

"I will if you will."

"What?"

"I'll ask Angela if she has a friend who could tag along."

"Wow, that makes me seem pathetic."

"Only because you are."

She glared and he gave her an innocent smile.

"We could help each other out," he said. "You'll keep me from talking about work all night and I'll keep you from stuffing your face like a pig in front of strangers."

"As long as I can be a pig at home with the leftovers."

"Of course," he patted her head.

"Fine," she muttered. "So how'd you meet?"

"She bumped into my trolley while I was checking out the cabbage."

"*Fascinating*. Something to write home about."

He took her teasing and promised to call Angela later.

When she pestered him, he called her right then and there and she was surprised as she was still in the store. She laughed and agreed to the date.

Mia was both pleased for him and slightly feeling a strange stuffiness in her chest.

Possibly coming down with a cold, she surmised.

The next Saturday, Mia was pacing outside Westley's room. She'd knocked over and over but he hadn't answered. She had gotten ready ages ago and she'd even bothered with putting on jeans.

"I'M COMING IN!" Mia yelled before she threw the door open.

Westley still hadn't answered and she'd assumed he was still asleep. They were going to be late if he was.

The shower wasn't running and she saw a lump on the bed.

With an evil grin, she jumped and launched herself onto the bed, elbow first.

When she landed heavily with nothing to break her fall but the soft bed, she lay there laughing.

The bathroom door was opened and steam billowed out.

Mia looked up, grin on her face and her mouth went dry.

Westley was in nothing but a towel, water was dripping off of his toned body, and his wet hair was slicked off of his face with a few strands hanging above his eye. She almost followed a drop making its way down his abs but she held onto her decency.

He folded his arms, leaning against the door frame. "Are you proud of yourself?"

Mia recovered quickly, covering her eyes. "Oh no, I'm *blind*."

"You're lucky I'm even in a towel."

She jumped off the bed; eyes tightly shut and waved, "Fine, fine I'm leaving."

She made her way to the door, her arms waving in front of her to feel it until she reached and touched something wet.

She frowned and pinched.

The sharp gasp she received made her shut her eyes even tighter.

"I uh… seem to have gone the wrong way huh?"

"Yes."

"Sorry about that."

"It's fine."

"I'll uh… just turn and leave."

"Maybe you should stop pinching my nipples first."

Mia's eyes shot open and she pulled her hands back like he'd burned her.

"That was an accident!"

He looked down at her in amusement and lifted her chin with a finger. "My eyes are up here."

Mia felt her face heat up and she spun around and hurried to the door.

"Hurry up!"

Westley laughed as he watched her go and turned to get dressed.

Minutes later, he was in the kitchen with her eating breakfast. She was pointedly talking about everything but her groping and he decided to have mercy on her and let it slide.

He was dressed in a simple black button down shirt and jeans.

He had invited Angela to the amusement park and had asked if she could bring someone along for a double date since he was bringing Mia.

She had seemed more than happy to.

When they got to the amusement park, Angela was waiting at the entrance.

"Hey, have you been here long?" he asked, greeting her. They weren't late but he hated to make a lady wait.

"No, we just got here," she said with a bright smile before she greeted Mia.

Westley had said the date would be a casual one to the amusement park but Angela had shown up in heels, jeans and a tight top. Beautiful, no doubt but the shoes would kill her.

She suspected Angela had wanted all eyes on her and she didn't think she was wrong.

"Mia, this is Terry."

Mia was pleasantly surprised. Terry was cute with light brown hair and brown eyes a shade darker than Angela's.

"Hey," he said, smiling shyly. "I would have brought flowers but thought it would be weird if you were allergic. Or had to carry them around an amusement park."

Mia laughed. "Good call."

He smiled and they all walked in, making small talk.

Terry was an old friend of Angela's. He was an actuary in an insurance firm and she was a psychoanalyst with her own practice.

They had breakfast first at a small café in order to get to know each other better.

When Angela tripped on a rock and Westley caught her, Mia suggested they get her some comfortable shoes, maybe slippers or something but the woman had been adamant and even a little annoyed at the suggestion and they'd all gone ahead and gone to the rides.

Her date was fine. He was smart and kind of cute but boring as hell. Mia refused to believe that this was the best single friend Angela could procure on short notice. She'd have had more fun going on a date with her gynaecologist and reminiscing about her pregnancy scares.

Also, she noticed that Terry would occasionally stare at Angela and she felt a small twinge of pity. He liked the other woman obviously, and there she was trying to fob him off on another woman.

It was cruel; especially because it was pretty obvious Terry had a thing for her.

When Westley and Angela went on the tea cup ride, Mia decided to stay behind and asked Terry of he wanted to grab a drink. He agreed and they sat at a nearby bench watching their two friends.

"You're in love with Angela," she said quietly.

To his credit, he didn't look surprised or even try to deny it. "Have been for the longest time."

"Does she know?"

"You met me five minutes ago and figured it out," he said good-naturedly.

She shrugged. "I'm a genius, that's all."

He chuckled. "She knows but all she wants is my friendship. I'm not hanging around her waiting for the day she changes her mind."

"Then what are you doing?"

"Meeting new people," he said, looking at her. "Don't worry; I do typically stay away from her. Being around the person you care about doesn't help you get over them."

She nodded, thinking of all the times she'd stayed in her and Eric's apartment when they broke up while he left to new and better places. And women.

"Are you in love with Westley?" he asked after a moment.

"Nah," she said. "I keep him around for his cooking."

He hummed, seeming to not quite believe her but she shrugged. It was true.

She saw Westley laugh at something Angela said and wondered why the fact that he was actually getting along with the other woman made her uncomfortable.

Westley and Angela walked to them and suddenly, Angela tripped.

Westley caught her before she could fall and she laughed easily until she realised she'd twisted her ankle.

Mia and Terry rushed to them and Terry bent to check her foot while she leaned on Westley. When he put pressure on it, she flinched and

Westley lifted her up, ignoring her protests. He carried her to the park's clinic and Mia took that time to admit to herself that she wasn't a bad match for Westley.

Angela was witty, smart and beautiful.

And she didn't gripe and groan when her ankle swelled, only flinching once or twice while the matron tended to it. She joked with Westley about suing him for her injuries and Mia felt a pang in her chest as he laughed.

They were getting along really well.

And she could admit, at least to herself, that she was a little jealous.

Angela was told to head home and put ice on it. The woman had come to the park with Terry and he assured them he'd get her home safe.

"I'm really sorry about this," Angela said to Westley, holding his hand.

"It's not like you planned to injure yourself," he replied. "Get well soon and next time we can do something safer. Like suffer through my cooking."

Her face brightened at that. "I'd love that. Is tomorrow night okay?"

153

"Will your leg be alright?"

She laughed. "Of course. I didn't break it. Would you rather not?"

"I'll pick you up at five. We can have a nice quiet dinner at my place."

She smiled and nodded and he let her go, waving at Terry.

Mia did her best to hype the date up on their way home. She teased Westley endlessly about it to mask her discomfort at having Angela over.

Westley hadn't asked her but that didn't mean he couldn't have someone over. So the next day, when he started making dinner, Mia helped even though she wanted to over salt everything for some reason.

"Do you like how she smiles? No one is that happy," she said, moving out of his way as he walked to the fridge.

Westley looked amused. "Really?"

She passed him the salt even though he'd already used it. "Really. She could be a serial killer. But don't let that stop you from engaging in a bit of coitus."

Westley only added a dash and smiled. The dish was done and Mia stared at it, her mouth watering from the smell alone. Lasagne and a pot roast. A fresh garden salad and so many sides and appetizers, it was like he was trying to fatten her up and force her to be too large to not stay the night.

"You are so getting laid tonight," she whispered.

Westley laughed and cuffed her upside her head. "Thank you. I think. I'm gonna go pick her up. I'll be back in thirty."

"I'll be out of your hair," she said.

"What? Why? You're eating with us."

"Um, what?" Mia blinked. "Are you dumb?"

He rolled his eyes. "It's dinner. You haven't eaten."

"I could eat now and-"

"Shut it. I'll see you soon."

He left without another word and she sat, confused.

When he got back, she opened the door and Westley blinked at her attire. She was dressed like a waiter.

"What the hell are you wearing?"

She ignored him and greeted Angela who was dressed in a simple sun dress and sandals. The swelling had gone down and her foot seemed fine though she was being gentle with it.

"Hey Angela," Mia greeted. "How's your leg?"

Angela seemed a little disappointed to see her. "Mia, hi. It's much better, thank you."

"Come in, I'll lead you both to the kitchen."

"Were you heading out?"

"No," Mia said with a laugh. "I'm your chaperone."

Angela raised an eyebrow at that and Westley grinned.

Dinner was great and Mia went to her room right after, feeling every bit the third wheel but hating that she'd left them alone. She heard the door open and close and wondered if Westley was going to Angela's house.

She also wondered why she felt the strange weight get off of her chest when she heard the door open again sometime later. It wasn't long enough that anything would have happened, she reasoned and then she slammed her head against her pillow.

What did it matter if he slept with Angela?

It was none of her business.

She slept fitfully that night.

Recipe for Denial

- Begin by throwing out the book on banting
- Reclaim your carbs
- Obtain 5 large Irish potatoes one way or another. Peeled and chopped up into small pieces
- 1 stick of butter
- ¼ cup milk
- 1 cup onion
- 600g mincemeat
- 2 cups carrots, baby corn, greenbeans – chopped
- 1 tablespoon Worcestershire sauce
- 2 tablespoon barbecue/steak sauce
- Salt, pepper, herbs and spices of your choice

- Boil potatoes about 20 to 30 minutes - until tender.
- Saute the vegetables in oil of choice. Add diced onions and cook for 5 to 10 minutes.
- Cook mincemeat in oil in separate pan. Season. Add salt, pepper and cooked vegetables.
- Add Worcestershire sauce and barbecue sauce
- Add water or ½ cup of beef broth. Simmer.
- Preheat oven to 200 degree Celsius.
- Mash cooked potatoes with 5 tablespoons of butter and milk. Mash until fluffy. Season with salt and pepper and mix.
- Spread meat in casserole dish. Cover with mashed potatoes.
- Bake for about 30 minutes – until browned and bubbling.

Note: Grandma Jo may not admit it but your version would definitely taste better than hers if you could cook.

Chapter 8: Recipe for Denial

-

The weeks passed slowly with Mia denying her growing feelings for Westley. He seemed to be seeing Angela at least three times a week, during his lunch-breaks. Mia had stopped denying that she was jealous and taken on extra work at her office.

Even though she thought it was better to avoid Westley altogether, she thought that would have made it too obvious given that he still spent his weekends at their house with her.

He cooked and she cleaned, they argued over TV shows and plot holes, they made loud noises when they saw their elderly neighbours standing near their hedges hoping to scare the old women into early graves...

They were friends and that should have been enough. She chalked up her feelings to a crush. Westley was hot. Baby blues, rugged form, five o'clock shadow begging to me rubbed against... Any normal human being would have started to wonder exactly what it would be like to actually *be* with him.

Westley seemed to like her well enough and they got along well, like a forest fire on the driest of her dad's jokes. They were friends and she couldn't deny that much anymore.

The problem was that when he walked in with his sweats and vest, her brain had an aneurysm. The problem was that when he tested out recipes and licked his lips thoughtfully, wondering whether to add soy sauce or Worchester sauce, she wanted to help him lick them.

She was obviously lusting after him so that meant it was probably nothing more than a crush.

And crushes went away.

She hoped.

When Westley told her they needed to go to the grocery store again, she should have listened to the advice in her head that sounded like Max's voice.

Max always said to dress like you were going to bump into your ex and wear underwear that wouldn't embarrass your mother if you were hit by a car and rushed to the emergency room.

Mia knew it would have happened eventually. She did.

She had just hoped it wouldn't have happened while she was in the most comfortable of Westley's t-shirts that she'd stolen from the fresh laundry and sweats that she suspected were also his because they were huge.

With how small Lusaka was, Mia was surprised Eric actually hadn't just moved in next door. Or been adopted by her parents or something.

Even so, knowing the microscopic properties of the capital didn't particularly help her out with being prepared to meet Eric out in the real world.

She thanked the Lord for her sudden seemingly fast metabolism; her only saving grace after months of eating Westley's cooking and looked forward with as much grace as one could when they looked like a freshly bathed hobo. She figured the stress from living with Wes had initially helped her keep from gaining even more weight.

There was her ex, standing at the fruit display, looking at his girlfriend's melons like he was vegan.

She considered changing directions but she'd be damned if she let Eric scare her off from getting sustenance. The fruit section was right before the bakery with the best red velvet cake that side of the continent.

She held her head high.

"Is there something on the ceiling?" Westley asked.

Maybe she'd held it a little too high. She gave Westley a dirty look.

"What?" he asked.

Mia sighed. It was too late to warn him and she didn't want to try.

However, Westley must have noticed too because he took her hand with a practised ease and stopped to pick up a canister of bug spray.

"How about this one?" he asked, as if he were presenting a diamond ring for her inspection.

Mia almost burst out into laughter and settled for an amused grin at his hopelessness.

"Hello, Mia," a voice said.

Mia steeled herself and turned. She widened her eyes in mock surprise and said, "Eric. Hello."

Westley looked at Eric and then at the woman next to him, a thin, young blond woman with a bright smile. He was willing to bet she was still in college.

The girl was looking at him with stars in her eyes.

"Oh my gosh, are you Westley Nott?" she asked, her voice an excited whisper. "Oh wow. *Wow*." She turned to Eric. "You didn't say you knew *Westley Nott*!"

"I don't know him," Westley said, eyebrow raised.

The girl didn't seem to hear because she'd turned to Mia.

"And you're *Mia*!" she said, taking Mia's free hand and shaking it vigorously like Mia was a war hero who had fought bravely for her country. "It's so nice to meet you. I've seen your pictures in the apartment. I was telling Eric it was weird that you're his best friend and your pictures are *everywhere* but you never visit. I was starting to think he'd made you up. Or that you were his ex or something…" she added with a laugh.

"*Us* dating?" Mia laughed drily with a look at Eric. "That would never happen."

There was a flash of indignation from Eric and Mia gave him a pitying smile, "You need to take those pictures down, Eric. This is embarrassing."

163

The blond laughed. "I'm Emily," she blushed as Eric pulled her closer. "Eric's girlfriend."

"Congratulations," Mia said with a smile. "He'd told me he found someone and was *so happy*."

"Aww babe," Emily said, kissing Eric's cheek.

Eric was smiling like he hadn't sent her any messages saying he wanted to try again. The ass was even squeezing his girlfriend closer like he hadn't left Mia voice mails saying he missed her and needed her to come back to him.

It was disgusting.

Mia realised Westley had moved closer to her and he and Eric had been watching each other the whole time.

"I'm glad you're making new friends," Eric said pleasantly, placing emphasis on 'friends' and then tugged Emily close again.

Westley chuckled goodnaturedly, "Oh, we're not *friends*," he said and that was all the warning Mia got before he pressed his lips to hers. Mia gasped in surprise but at the gentle, insistent pressure, her eyes closed a moment later and she let out a heady sigh. Westley kissed her slowly, gently, like he'd used up all their passion that morning and this was them basking in the afterglow.

He nibbled on her bottom lip and she pressed back harder against him before she remembered herself and pulled away, her face warm and flushed.

She didn't take her eyes off of Westley and his gaze was focussed on her like he was going to kiss her again – and more – location be damned.

"Wow..."

Both of them turned, surprised, and found themselves looking at Emily's flushed face. The blonde let out a shaky breath and giggled.

Eric looked like he'd just eaten something sour and he said, "I suppose time and place were never your forte."

Mia put a restraining hand on Westley when she saw his jaw clench and she gave Eric a grin. "And cradle robbing was always yours."

Before Eric could say anything else, Mia said, "We'll let you two finish your shopping."

Mia waved as the couple walked passed them, Eric not sparing her another glance but kissing Emily behind her ear the way he used to do to Mia.

Mia was silent the rest of their time at the store and couldn't have gotten home quickly enough.

"Are you okay?" Westley asked the moment they walked through the door, when he thought it was safe.

She spun on him. "Eric is dating some model and I'm playing wingman for you and Angela. Of course I'm *okay!*"

"I didn't force you to play wingman," he responded calmly.

"I know you didn't," she said irritably and then sighed. "I shouldn't have gone out today."

"So you could stay here and do *what*? Never leave the house again in case you see your ex?" Westley asked, annoyed despite himself.

"Just leave me alone," she mumbled.

"What *exactly* is your plan?" Westley demanded. "Stare at Eric's pictures on your phone and jump the moment he says he wants you back?

Is that what you were hoping he'd do today even after he so obviously flaunted his new girl in front of you?"

Mia frowned, "You don't know what you're talking about."

"Really? Isn't that what you do?" he asked mockingly. "Take him back after he's done whoring? And learn to appreciate all the new things his new toys taught him?"

Mia swung but he caught her hand easily.

"Why are you angry with me when you treat yourself like you have no standards? You still want to be with him?" he asked, his surprise obvious in his anger. "Are you *serious* right now?"

"Fuck off, Westley."

"I can't believe you," he murmured.

"Leave me alone," she whispered, tugging her hand.

"Like hell," he said. "Why are you so determined to go back to someone who treats you like crap?"
"I'm not!" she insisted.

"Then why are you so angry?"

"Because I'm stuck!" she exploded. "He was the *only* person I'd ever loved and he's able to move on at a moment's notice while I'm always just... stuck. My life hasn't changed since he dumped me. It's the same!"

Westley waited for her to continue and she did.

"He said we were meant to be together and I know he treated me like crap. I *know*! I'm not stupid, Westley!" Her voice cracked. "I'm *not* stupid."

She shut her eyes and tried to tug her hand from his grasp but he pulled her into his arms.

"I want to believe I deserved better," she whispered weakly, stiff in his embrace. "But if he loved me…If he *said* he loved me and treated me that way… What if I never find someone who…"

"Mia," he said, holding her tightly as she finally broke down.

He sat her down on the couch, pulling her onto his lap and rocking her back and forth and he spoke.

"He's a bastard and you didn't deserve any of it," he said, holding her close. "You get to decide how you let people treat you. That includes Eric and whoever else you'll be with after him."

Mia could almost see the self-help books and motivational posters in her head and was glad he didn't quote them at her right that moment. Leah had already gifted her sets of them. It was one thing to know what to do and quite another to do it. But she felt that she was making progress.

Westley wiped her face and handed her a tissue to blow her nose.

Then he put on some old movies and broke out the ice-cream.

When she laughed, he said defensively, "It's what my mom did for me after my first girlfriend dumped me."

"When was that?" she asked with a sniff.

"Kindergarten," he replied wistfully. "It was the best recess of my life and then she went off and kissed Joey Martin from first grade."

"That hussy," Mia chuckled. "You deserved better."

He nodded. "I really did."

They talked through the whole movie and she talked about how she met Eric.

"He bumped into me and apologized. It was very meet-cute," she said with a roll of her eyes.

As she told him all about her relationship with Eric, its ups and countless downs, Westley rubbed her back, holding her to his side.

When she'd been quiet for a few minutes, having run out of steam, Westley said, "What are you thinking right now?"

"That I don't love him," she said tiredly. "I just got so used to the idea that no one else could love me properly," she said with a laugh. "It's silly. I know it for the manipulation it is but when you're home alone eating shrimp-flavoured ramen and the text comes in saying 'I made a huge mistake' and he's outside with flowers and chocolates, wine and teddy bears… you start to think that maybe it's better being with him."

"You only thought that because the ramen was shrimp-flavoured." Mia shoved him and he laughed and pulled her to his side.

"You deserve the best, Mia," he said. "You're an amazing woman. Do you understand me?"

"No."

Westley chuckled. "Terry's a nice guy, if a little boring."

"How dare you. Actuarial science is actually *fascinating* once you skim the Wikipedia page," she said.

170

Westley pretended to doze off and she smacked his arm.

"I will say this," Westley said. "I've sort of missed you bugging me recently. You're always busy. Or off meeting Terry."

"I'm surprised you even notice when you're always off with Angela," she countered.

"At least I like Angela. You're the one hanging out with an actuary you don't even like," he scoffed.

"First off, I like Terry. And we only had coffee alone a few times. He's good company. Second, so what if you like Angela?"

She hadn't meant it to come off as harsh as it did and from the surprise on Westley's face, he hadn't either but she didn't stop. "This isn't a competition. Who cares if you like her?"

They were silent for a few seconds, watching each other and then Westley said, "You do, apparently."

"Oh please. I don't give a shit," she said, standing up off the couch.

Westley followed her. "Really."

She spun around and gave him a mirthless smile. "Yup. After all, nothing has changed. I still hate you."

He snorted. "No but you wish you did."

Mia shook her head at him, her irritation robbing her of her words. She made to walk passed him and would have but he blocked her way.

"You care."

"Get away from me, Westley."

"Tell me you care," he said softly.

She scoffed. "Why? Did Angela say it'll help me-"

"Mia."

She looked up at him in suspicion. *"What?"*

"I care about you," he said resignedly.

She rolled her eyes.

"Yes, yes, we're great friends and I am eternally grateful," she said in a mocking tone. "Now would you get the hell-"

She'd turned, in true dramatic fashion, ready to twist around him when she'd slipped on an upturned corner of the carpet. She tumbled and he went down with her, the same traitorous carpet taking them both down.

Westley broke her fall and groaned, turning them so they were both on their sides.

"I'm sorry, are you okay?" she whispered in horror.

His arms were still around her and hers were braced lightly on his chest.

"Westley-"

"Shut up for a moment, woman," he hissed.

Mia shut up and didn't move, watching him with worry.

He opened his eyes and seemed to realise just how close they were.

"Are you okay?" he asked and she nodded quietly.

A stray curl found its way to her cheek and he brushed it away.

Her brown eyes widened in surprise and he looked at her.

"You're impossible."

She scoffed. "I-"

"Be quiet a little longer," he said, moving closer.

Mia took in a sharp breath. She could feel his heart beating faster beneath her palms.

"Wes-"

He kissed her then, softly. Just a light brush of his lips against hers.

He moved back and looked at her. His eyes searched her face and his hands were on her waist, slowly pressing her to him. When his lips met hers again, Mia hesitated for all of three seconds before she responded.

He tasted like quietly burning passion, warmth and fire, barely restrained desire and just a hint of vanilla. Mia felt off kilter and wrapped her hands around his neck to keep her balance. Westley's tongue grazed her lips, once, twice, begging for entrance and she moaned, parting her lips to allow it. She moaned at the feel of him, at the *want* he brought out in her. Eric had certainly never kissed her that way.

Westley drew her closer and her breasts were flush against his chest. He whispered something against her lips and she barely had the presence of mind to ask him what it was. She felt it didn't matter. What mattered was that he didn't stop.

It was intoxicating.

"I want you," Westley said, backing away for a moment. "Should we stop?"

Mia brushed her lips against his and revelled in the power she felt when he shut his eyes for a moment as if to gather himself.

"No, but afterward," she said. "We have to go back to normal."

Westley raised an eyebrow at that. "Of course."

Mia knew they sounded like idiots.

And liars.

"Back to hating each other," she said and he captured her lips in a heated kiss.

Her brain provided her with some vital information when it decided to restart. She tore her lips away from Westley's. "Wait, no."

At his surprised look, she said, "Angela."

Westley seemed confused for a moment like he didn't know what she was talking about so she said again, "Um... Angela?"

"What about her?"

"What do you mean?" she asked, bristling. "Aren't you two-"

Realization came to him and he laughed. "What? No. I wasn't seeing her on dates. I hired her to be my psychotherapist."

Mia blinked. "Seriously? Didn't that upset her?"

"For those fees, I imagine the money will help her heal," he said, pulling her hand and tugging her back to him. "She said I was attached to you and you to me and suggested we work it out somehow."

He led her to the couch and pulled her onto his lap, her legs to either side of him.

"Is this working it out?" Mia asked, sitting carefully in his lap, knowing the friction might undo what was left of her control.

Westley kissed her jawline. "It's working for me."

"Westley..." she moaned.

"What?" he asked, lips pressed lightly against her soft skin.

176

"What are we doing?"

He paused. "Do you want to stop?"

"Is that what I said?" she asked.

He laughed and kissed her, claiming her mouth and leaving no part of it untouched by his tongue in slow, hungry kisses.

"Nothing's changed," she said, trying to convince herself.

He nodded, licking her neck. "Nothing at all."

"This means nothing," she said breathily.

Westley squeezed her ass and pulled her sharply to him so their bodies were pressed against each other. He ground into her and she moaned.

Mia kissed him with fervour, savouring the flavour of his mouth as her fingers got started on his shirt.

"If things get complicated," Mia said against his lips. "We can just...stop."

"And if your ex comes back to you?" he asked.

"I'll take him back without a second thought," she grinned at his incredulous expression and said. "I'm kidding."

"This could end badly," Westley said, eyes on her bare breasts and more than a little distracted.

Mia nodded and ground slowly on him. "Yes but do you really care about that right now?"

He did not. "Do you?"

"I still hate you."

"Is that why you're having sex with me right now?"

"I couldn't think of a better way to say it up close."

He was getting tired of her being able to form coherent sentences.

"Is this even sex yet?" she asked, her chuckle turning to a gasp as he sucked at her pulse. "I mean-"

"My wiener is not in your cavern of doom?"

"Cavern of doom, I like it."

"Are you always this talkative during sex?" he asked, biting her.

"Only when my mouth isn't busy so I guess-" He covered her mouth with his, stopping her rambling.

Westley studied every inch of her skin, first with his eyes and then with his fingers, unable to keep himself from touching her.

If he only got this chance, this one time, he would ensure they wouldn't regret it.

He lifted Mia and placed her on the couch. He kept his mouth firmly on hers, exploring and ravenous.

His caresses were reverent, roaming the smooth flesh beneath his hands, his fingers lightly touching her in some places and massaging her in others, until she was shivering from it. His mouth joined in the exploration of her breasts, massaging them and letting his lips, teeth and tongue seek out the dark nipples.

Mia groaned, holding his head tighter to her as he sucked hard and let his fingers roam lower, lathering her with attention, making her squirm and gasp. She was still in her jeans and his shirt was half way undone.

It wasn't fair.

Mia put her hands on his shoulders and pushed him back. He came up, eyes heavy lidded and questioning and she knew if she asked him to stop right then, even though he wanted her just as much as she wanted him, he would have stopped.

Mia kissed him and moved off the couch. He went with it and smiled against her lips when she spun them around and pushed him onto the carpeted floor. They attacked their clothes then, barely breaking apart from their kisses for too long, groaning and gasping when they brushed against sensitive areas and needed it to happen again.

Mia shrugged out of her jeans, kicking them off next to Westley's. She climbed over and straddled his strong thighs, her hair spilling over her shoulders. For a moment they paused, staring at each other.

Westley had imagined having Mia like this a million times but nothing could compare to the reality of her. Everything in his body was tensed, balancing on the edge of something he wasn't sure he was quite ready to fall off of yet.

Mia shifted on Westley's lap, enough to get better access to his mouth but the simple movement rubbed his groin against hers and Westley took in a sharp breath.

The gleam in her light brown eyes seemed to imply she liked the sound of that and in the next moment, she ground down slowly on him, causing Westley to groan at the feel of it. She was wet, and deliciously so, sliding easily over his cock, back and forth.

Her breaths came in shallow gasps and he gripped her hips, slowing her down even more. He didn't want it to end just yet and he wasn't quite ready to be sent over the edge.

He wanted her to be halfway out of her mind by the time things got *really* interesting.

Westley grabbed her waist and tugged. Mia looked at him in confusion for a moment before she realised what he wanted her to do and her face warmed.

He noted her reaction and grinned, not giving her any more time to think it over, he lifted her thighs and quickly slid down the length of her, until his mouth was below her.

Westley wasted no time before soaking up his victory by nudging her thighs open a little wider. Mia held her breath, meeting his eyes and then closing hers when he slicked his tongue across her velvety heat.

Westley wasted no time devouring her and he felt her body react like an electric shock pulsed through her.

Mia was lost in the sensation. Her head was thrown back and her eyes were shut tightly against the pressure building in her groin. Her hand went to his hair, diving into the dark strands and holding on.
She didn't notice Westley sliding his hand over her hips and behind her. A finger tenderly caressed her entrance and her eyes flew open with a start. She opened her eyes and looked down at Westley. His blue eyes had darkened with lust and he was watching her. The sight of him so eagerly pleasing her nearly drove her mad. She was so worked up.

Her breathing came laboriously with deep moans punctuating each puff of air while Westley pleasured her with his tongue and a finger.

She was so close to exploding that when a second finger entered her, Mia tugged at Westley's tousled hair to warn him that his orgasm was eminent. But Westley didn't budge, speeding up his movements, licking and sucking, revelling in how her hips were moving sensuously against him, how she buried her hands in his hair as she held his mouth to her.

When her climax took her, Mia couldn't do anything but moan out a steady stream of whispered words, some of which sounded like his name, as her whole body shivered. It was the sexiest litany of curses Westley had ever heard and he couldn't help the lecherous smirk that graced his features when Mia, flushed and sated, opened her eyes.

Westley's tongue darted out as he licked his lips, already wet from her and Mia felt her insides tighten against the fingers that he'd left stroking lazily in her. It was almost enough to forgive him all the things he'd done to her.

Almost.

Her face burned, in pleasure and embarrassment, and she looked ready to bolt.

Westley took that moment to lift her in a smooth motion and slide up before pulling her down to him and kissing her. Her taste was sweet and heavy and he pressed his tongue into her mouth. She made a needy sound that went straight to his groin and his fingers dug into her waist.

Mia didn't ask where he'd magicked a condom from but her soft hands slid over his as he put it on all while kissing her leisurely.

He was large. It wasn't that she had personally a lot to compare him to, because there really was no contest between him and Eric- her ex would find himself lacking, but she liked to think her internet history was proof she'd at least studied what was average and what- wasn't.

Westley deepened their kiss as he rolled her over. His hands roamed everywhere, her back, his, breasts, stomach, any place he could reach. Mia grasped him as he took in a sharp breath, barely holding back a groan as she stroked him slowly.

Westley settled between her knees and lowered his chest to hers, loving the feel of her breasts against his skin. Her skin was so soft.

Having her beneath him, ebony waves strewn across the carpet beneath them, her gorgeous naked body waiting, he hesitated again.

Mia gave him a tiny impatient glare; opening her legs wider for him and pulling him back down to kiss her. He kissed her hungrily, sucking on her tongue and drawing out a gasp from her, as he pushed inside until he was buried deep.

She felt amazingly hot and tight and when she wrapped her legs around his waist, somehow pushing him impossibly deeper, he groaned.

They began to move in slow, tentative strokes, finding their rhythm.

"I won't break, y'know," Mia managed to say, pressing on the back of his hips to give him permission to thrust harder. He took it.

Westley slid his hands beneath her hips and lifted, angling her so she could take him in deeper. A hand came up to cup her breast and she arched and moaned as he gently rolled her nipple between his fingers, teasing the hard nub.

She gasped and dug her fingernails into his lower back, as he plowed into her as hard as he could.

"*Don't stop*," Mia groaned, her body thrummed in ecstasy, drawing out the word as she fought with her body to be patient and not rush to the end.

Westley was whispering a reverent chant as he picked up his pace, Mia's name ghosting across his lips with each slam of his hips.

He didn't know if it was the strangled cry of his own name from her lips, the tightening of her muscles as she came, or a combination of both,

185

but Westley didn't last much longer before he groaned out and bit roughly into her shoulder.

He collapsed on top of her, breathing in the sweet scent of her shampoo and she ran her hands lightly over his back as she shuddered, her body still experiencing tiny shocks of pleasure long after her orgasm had passed.

Silence grew between them as they both stared at each other, brown watching blue, catching their breath. "I don't suppose we could try this again?" Westley asked, putting on a mask of casual indifference. "To make sure we really hate each other."

Mia pursed her lips to keep from smiling. "Well, I suppose it would be the right thing to do," she reasoned. "Just to be sure."

"It helps that we would be much too tired after to even try disrupting any future events Leah hosts," he said.

"That's a good point," Mia replied with mock seriousness. "And Leah was going on and on about how we should try to get along."

"I'd say we're getting along swimmingly," Westley gave her a sexy grin before capturing her mouth with his again and seeing to it that they continued to get along the rest of the day.

Recipe for Desire

- The most moist, decadent and *delicious* chocolate cake you have ever tasted with frosting that could only lead you to hell after a taste of heaven.
- There is no way on earth you can make it.
- Buy it from Grandma Jo.

Chapter 9: Recipe for Desire

-

Mia sat straight-faced through the most boring early morning meeting of her life. She didn't mind numbers but she felt like she'd not heard words that didn't have 'percent' and 'dollars' attached to the end of them in over three hours.

She resisted glaring at her boss, May, CEO and evil overlord of the firm who knew no one enjoyed getting up at 6 to hear what they were doing right and know how they could improve. Most meetings that served the sole purpose of berating them and telling them how they'd messed up were reserved for the later hours of the night. May seemed to think depriving her employees of sleep when they fucked up was a suitable punishment.

The financial manager finally stopped speaking and it took a moment for Mia to realise May had asked her a question but her years of absently listening to her parents lecturing her made her prepared and she repeated the sentence like she'd been paying the utmost attention.

"What do I think of the report?" she looked down at it thoughtfully. "We are doing well but we can always do better."

May smiled sweetly and asked, "How?"

Mia wanted to throw her pen at her mentor. The woman knew she hadn't been paying attention and was bored out of her mind.

"Well, obviously we need to-"

A sudden knock at the door made them all turn. Mia's secretary, Nancy gave them all an apologetic smile.

"Excuse me, I'm sorry to disturb you all but a client just walked in requesting Miss Rhodes," she said.

May's policy on business was straightforward. Anyone, from interns to the CEO could disturb a meeting if it was for a client. That was where their pay checks came from after all.

Mia nodded and left the conference room, glad for the reprieve.

Nancy was a bright young woman still studying to take the bar exam. She grinned at her boss. "You look happy to escape."

"If you made up a client to get me out of there," Mia said. "I'm proposing immediately."

"Sorry but no," Nancy laughed. "I want to know how you landed him as a client though."

"Sorry?"

Nancy nudged her as they approached her office. The blinds were down so she couldn't see into it and she liked it that way.

When Nancy just nodded at the door, Mia shrugged and opened it.

Then shut it and turned to face Nancy.

"He's eating my snacks. Did you let him eat my snacks?"

Nancy looked at her incredulously. "He's Westley Nott. He *is* a snack."

"Hardly nutritious," she muttered and Nancy gave her a pointed look.

Mia sighed and walked into her office, shutting the door behind her and leaning against it.

Westley smiled at her and said nothing as he had another crisp.

"I'm charging you per word," she said. "And you're officially a new client."

Westley got up. "I could possibly afford to do that but conflict of interest."

"What conflict?" she asked, looking up at him as he reached her.

"My interest," he said, pressing her to the door and letting her know, for emphasis, what exact part was interested.

Westley leaned down and gently captured her lips in a sweet kiss. When he found no resistance – he'd been expecting her to tell him this wasn't proper office use- he deepened the kiss, opening his lips when he felt Mia's tongue run across them.

She kissed him leisurely and he relaxed into it. He raised a hand to her chin briefly before letting his fingers trail down her neck and along her collarbone. When her only reaction was to moan softly and press closer, he continued his languid exploration. He moved back into to go lower and lick at her exposed neck.

Mia gasped, arching, her hands coming up to run through his hair. Westley nipped and sucked at her neck, soothing his sharp bites with gentle sweeps of his tongue. Westley's hands moved to focus on unbuttoning her prim white button-down shirt but when she tried to touch him he shooed her hands.

"Don't distract me," he said against her skin and she shivered.

Mia's breathing became more uneven as Westley worked his way down once her bra was exposed. He caressed her nipples through the fabric, ignoring the sounds of her wanting him to get rid of the bra. He had pushed her shirt to her shoulders but hadn't removed it.

He delved his tongue into her navel and Mia let out a high sound. He shushed her and her shaky hands came to rest on his shoulders.

Westley kissed lower still, soft wet kisses that left her skin tingling across her waistline.

Westley hiked up her skirt, exposing her even further. His hands went to her thighs and she shivered when she felt his hot breath against her inner thigh. He made her make more room for him, spreading her legs. Her whole body tensed in anticipation as he kissed around the place she wanted him to go the most.

When she gripped his head and whimpered her complaint, Westley took pity on her and let his tongue run over the lacy fabric of her panties.

Mia let out a low breath, her hips bucking forward, unconsciously seeking more contact with Westley's tongue.

Westley helped her out of her panties and went right back in.

His tongue was firm and insistent, almost punishingly slow and Mia felt that she would sob if he kept teasing her. His tongue swirled along her slit, teasing her without mercy. When he felt her muscles tighten, he groaned and Mia shuddered at the vibrations from it.

Westley's hands moved round to cup her ass and Mia almost cried out loud when he suddenly put more pressure against her clit. She gasped out his name and started to ride his face, spurred on by his encouraging moans and the way he was kneading her ass and guiding her hips in their sensual back and forth, serpentine-smooth movements.

She writhed in anticipation and when he suddenly sucked hard, insistently, on her clit, she cried out, her hands curling in his hair. Her orgasm rolled over her in waves and she bucked above him as he lapped her up, driving her orgasm on as she continued to thrust against his mouth.

Westley continued to lick her, gently, letting her convulse with the aftershocks of her orgasm. She groaned heavily, almost collapsing against the door. He caught her easily and pressed her back to the door, kissing her and letting her taste herself on his tongue.

She sighed contentedly and reached down to his bulge. He was huge against her hand and he moaned when she squeezed, enjoying the delicious feel of it.

However, when her fingers went to his zipper, he stilled her hands.

"Uh uh," he managed to say, his voice seeming strangled.

"But," she frowned. "You haven't-"

"This one was for you," he said, pulling away and kissing her hair. "I live for the torment. Besides, I have to hurry back for a meeting."

"Okay-"

He smiled down at her. "Let's go out to lunch," he said. "There's a nice place near my building."

"*Or* we could order pizza and eat here," she suggested slyly.

"I'll need more than cheese to keep up with you," he said, kissing the corner of her mouth.

Mia smiled. "Fine. I still have my meeting though."

He grinned, slow and sexy. "Good luck concentrating. I'll send you the location."

She sighed when he adjusted himself and pressed a cold bottle of water to his crotch before he walked out. Nancy came in almost immediately, looking at his butt as he walked off.

"I hope you gave that a squeeze for me," she said looking impressed.

"What? Why would you think-"

Nancy cut her off with a look. "The walls may be soundproof but your hickey is quite... loud."

Mia groaned about the 'territorial bastard' and Nancy helped her cover it up.

"The meeting ended by the way," Nancy said, adding more foundation to Mia's neck.

Mia stayed still while her secretary fixed her up and then picked up her phone.

Westley had already sent her the location.

She smiled.

"My lips are sealed," Nancy said and then added as she walked out. "Tonight, my boyfriend starts doing squats."

Mia waved her off and heard a buzz from her phone. Thinking it was Wes, she opened her messages and stared.

'Hey, I think we need to talk about us'.

It was Eric.

She frowned at the message and deleted it, deciding to ignore it.

Leah would have been proud of her.

She worked till it was almost noon, burying herself in reports and trying her best not to think about Westley. Or his smile. Or his body. Or his mouth...

Mia drove to the location Westley sent her and surprisingly found a parking spot even during lunch hour. She dialled his line and drummed absently on her steering wheel.

"Hey, I'm here."

"I'll be right down," he said.

Mia heard the smile in his voice and found herself smiling as well. She snorted at her behaviour and looked at the large buildings outside. The place looked familiar and when she realised why, she groaned.

The Nott building was right next to Max's office building. Max was head of advertising at a large company and took his time seriously. He worked efficiently and *never* stayed over the time written on his contract. Nine to five did not mean nine to five thirty. And lunch hour meant lunch *hour*.

But, she knew, the chances of him seeing her weren't necessarily high. There were lots of cars there.

She got back to her phone, checking her afternoon meetings and almost jumped out of her skin when someone tapped on the glass.

Expecting to see Wes, she looked up and laughed when instead she found Max there, wearing a knowing look.

Mia put away her phone and got out the car.

"Hey," Max said pleasantly. "What are you doing here?"

"Hello to you too," Mia chuckled. "I'm waiting for Wes."

"You don't say," he said, grinning widely. "What for?"

"He's helping me with something so I came to get him."

"I'll bet he is," Max said with a smirk.

He stared at her and Mia kept her smile as neutral as possible. "Yes so-"

"Where is he going to *help* you?" Max asked.

"At lunch, I suppose. He may need to work with my company and offered his input."

"I'll bet he did."

"Will you make everything I say perverted?" Mia asked with a sigh.

"Yes," he replied. "Besides, we all know something is going on. Why not admit it?"

"Because nothing is going on and you're being an idiot?"

Max smirked. "Well, I imagine the secretive nature of your sordid affair keeps it interesting."

Mia gave up and settled for frowning at him.

"Well, I'll let you get on with your rendezvous," he winked. "And by the way... you smell like sex."

Mia gaped and looked down at her clothes as if her eyes could see scents.

Max laughed. "Too easy. Have fun!"

He waved and sauntered off while she glared at his back, hoping he tripped.

"Was that Max?" Westley said, coming up to her.

She nodded and then turned to look up at him. He looked just as good as he had earlier and the sunlight in his hair made her want to run her hands through it again.

He smiled and her face grew warm, remembering where his mouth had been a short while before.

"Hungry?" he asked, voice husky.

She cleared her throat. "For food. Starving."

He laughed at her response and led her away from both buildings.

"Is it far?" she asked.

"No, just at the corner," he said.

She saw it when he pointed. A tiny bistro that looked packed.

"Will we be able to find seats?" she asked doubtfully.

"You can sit on me-"

She punched his side and he coughed, holding back his laughter.

They got into the bistro and a young girl of about sixteen rushed up to them. Her braids swung as she walked and she stopped in front of Westley with an irritated look.

"Westley! I almost gave your table to an old woman who was dead on her feet."

Westley looked scandalized. "Why would you even think of giving someone else my spot?"

The girl sighed. "You know how I feel about making the old unhappy. She could've been a witch."

"Old age doesn't give you magic powers," Westley said and patted her head before turning her to face Mia. "Mwape, this is Mia. Mia, this is my cousin, Mwape."

Mwape gave Mia a wide smile. "Nice to meet you. You have the same name as some woman he was complaining about a while ago-"

Westley covered her mouth. "Ah, kids. They mishear death threats and rude names all the time."

Mia looked amused. "Uh huh."

They were led to the farthest corner of the restaurant and Mia realised it was a private booth, complete with a sliding door.

Mwape waved at them and said a waitress would come take their order cause her shift was over and she didn't care if they lose his business. They had to leave the door open though.

Westley insulted her work ethic as she hurried off.

"She seems nice," Mia chuckled.

"Yeah," he replied.

They sat and Westley whispered, "Hike up your skirt."

"What?"

"Now," he practically growled and she raised an eyebrow at him.

"Now, *please*," he amended and she smiled and slowly lifted her skirt. The table was high and the thick tablecloth would see to it that even if the booth door was open, no one would see a thing.

"Beautiful," Westley said, eyeing her thighs like a hungry man. "Now, scoot over."

Mia did as he said, scooting to the end of their booth's couch. She gasped when he put his hand to her ass and gave it a light squeeze.

The waitress came to them suddenly and Mia sat back just as suddenly in her surprise, Westley made a choked sound and she moved forward slightly. She picked up the menu, looking like an excited and hungry customer eager to order.

The waitress was smiling pleasantly though she looked exhausted. "Can I get you something to drink before you order or do you already know what you'd like?"

Mia hesitated as Wes's hand went further down. She lowered the large menu and used it to hide her face partly.

"I'll have orange juice," she said and cleared her throat.

Westley hummed, looking at her menu and leaning closer.

His fingers rubbed at her lightly and she tried not to shift toward or away from them.

"What did I have last time?" he asked the waitress.

She smiled in amusement and said, "You ordered a whole bottle of whiskey and your cousin spilled it all on the floor and called your mother."

"Is she here?"

"She just left."

"Then that's no fun. I'll have a coke."

She nodded. "And to eat or would you like more time?"

Mia bit her lip before saying, "What would you suggest?"

Westley's fingers moved her panties to the side and he slid one lightly over her clit.

"Our lemon and herb chicken is really good," the waitress said with a heavy nod. "It's the best this side of town."

Westley's finger slid into her and she nodded at the waitress' suggestion, staring hard at the menu.

"Lemon and herb chicken sounds wonderful. I'll have that."

"And you, sir?"

"I'll have the usual."

The waitress nodded and left.

Mia squirmed then, trying to get him to go deeper.

"So you come here often?" she asked, trying to keep her voice low. Was that where he took all his women?

He nodded. "At least three times a week. It's the first time I've brought someone with me, though. I try keep it secret from even my colleagues. Don't want anyone stealing my booth and eating my steak."

She nodded and his finger went in deeper. "I'm sure they have more than one steak in the kitchen."

"We don't know that for certain," he said, sliding his finger in and out of her.

She opened her legs wider and leaned forward further to give him better access. Westley sped up and bit his lip, watching her fuck herself on his fingers until she whimpered, gripping the table cloth and dropping her head to the table.

She caught her breath and got an evil glint in her eye.

"You can't..." he said and she ignored him.

Wes was looking a little too smug at having just made her cum and she slipped under the table abruptly. He was about to ask her if she was going to take a nap down there when he felt her hands on his belt.

"Whoa, the waitress will be back with our food-"

She shushed him. "Tell her I'm in the bathroom."

He wondered if he'd even be able to speak but his own response was cut off by a sharp intake of breath when Mia massaged him through his trousers.

His trousers were deftly unbuttoned and Mia's hand slipped inside. He tried to keep his eyes open but he knew he was fighting a losing battle. He grabbed the menu and held it up, his eyes fluttering shut the next moment when he felt her swipe the flat of her tongue across the head of his cock. Mia teased him like he'd done her. She stroked him and dragged her tongue up his rigid length from base to tip before lingering at the head against, swirling her tongue around the sensitive flesh.

She licked his shaft again and again until he was slick and her hand could easily slide up and down, and then she took him, all of him, into her mouth.

"Fuck..."

His moan made Mia want to pleasure him even more. She took him in her mouth and cupped his balls.

The table shook as he edged off of his seat, instinctively craving more of the pleasure she was plying onto him.

Mia sucked, and stroked and teased until he was practically growling and he dropped the menu, placing his hands in her hair, roughly letting it loose but not guiding her. He held on tight, his hips moving forward, almost off the edge of the sear as she brought him closer.

"*Mia*, don't stop," he groaned.

She didn't.

Mia loved his reactions and her own body was responding and she couldn't believe this was something she was doing.

Westley felt so incredibly hot. He wanted nothing more than to shove the table aside and plunge into Mia freely but he let her do what she wanted. The warm, wet heat of her mouth was incredible and he needed *more.*

Mia hummed around his cock before letting him thrust deep, the head of his cock brushing against the back of her throat. She swallowed convulsively to keep herself from gagging. Mia felt him swell impossibly larger against her tongue, not knowing how amazing her contracting throat had felt around his cock. She squeezed tighter as he whispered her name in a harsh warning as he came, losing control completely and giving himself over to his orgasm.

Westley hissed out a curse as Mia swallowed every hot drop, continuing to stroke and suck until his shudders stopped.

Mia put him back into his trousers once she'd licked him clean and then crawled up from under the table. Westley pulled her to him, kissing her long and deep and telling her she was amazing, beautiful and *going to pay*.

She giggled and pulled away at that last one.

Westley sighed and put his head on the table, a faint smile on his face.

The waitress came in a minute later with their food.

She glanced at Westley, whose head was still on the table and gave Mia a questioning glance.

"He's really excited about the steak," Mia explained.

The waitress nodded and placed their food in front of them after telling Westley to get his head off of their good tablecloth.

-

Recipe for Love

- Select preferred ingredients

- Create your own recipe

Chapter 10: Recipe for Love

-

To say that Mia was surprised at seeing Leah at her office would have been an understatement. It wasn't that it had never happened before; it was just that with how busy the other woman was lately, it was surprising to see her there.

There was, of course, also the fact that Max must have told Leah he'd seen her.

Leah sat on the large comfortable couch in Mia's room, taking off her shoes and reclining. Nancy brought her a cup of tea and she thanked her.

"Please, come in, make yourself at home," Mia said drily.

Leah smiled. "I was in the neighbourhood and thought I'd come say hello to my best friend."

"Would it be offensive for me to ask what you want before or *after* you finish your tea?"

"Either one is fine," Leah said, taking a sip. "But I really *was* in the neighbourhood. Your company hired me for a Heritage day bash."

Mia realised there'd been talks of that and she hadn't been interested. "Ah, I must have missed that. Congratulations?"

Leah waved her hand dismissively. "Don't worry about it. I actually thought this would be a good time to see you and invite you over."

"Invite me to my company's party?"

"To my house, smartass," she replied. "I haven't seen you in forever."

"I attend most of your events," Mia stated, eyebrow raised.

"You know what I mean," Leah said, giving her a dry look. "When was the last time we hung out just the two of us?"

Mia remembered it clearly and apparently so did Leah because she immediately said, "Sorry, I didn't mean to remind you of that."

The last time they'd been together alone had been when Leah had been comforting her over Eric's latest "it's not you it's me, I just need some time" generic break ups.

"It's fine, really," Mia said, relieved that that was true.

"Okay, so my place this weekend. We can go shopping before to stock up on snacks."

"And Lehmann?" Mia asked.

Leah smiled. "He gets kicked out. I'm sure he'll love some time to himself without me mumbling about plans."

"One day he'll reveal how much he truly hates me," Mia said with a laugh.

Leah grinned. "Yeah probably. How have you been though? I feel like you haven't complained about Wes in over two weeks. Is he dead?"

Mia blinked, wondering if Max had told Leah he'd seen her and tacked on his suspicions. She doubted it, though. Leah was much too straightforward to find a roundabout way of asking her if she'd had lunch with Westley. Still, it wouldn't hurt to be careful and see what she knew so Mia eloquently said, "Huh?"

Leah rolled her eyes. "Westley Nott. Bane of your existence. Housemate."

"He should really get all that onto a business card."

"It *is* pretty catchy," Leah said.

"You saw us getting along at your last charity," Mia said in answer to her question.

Leah frowned. "Yeah but I thought you were fake-behaving out of the kindness of your hearts because you didn't want Max to bankrupt me." "You two really need to stop betting on us," Mia admonished.

"It's so *addictive*," Leah whispered.

Mia threw an eraser at her friend who caught it easily and stood up.

"I should get going," Leah said, standing up and slipping on her shoes. "Don't want to get fired. My boss can be a real bitch."

"You're your own boss."

"Exactly."

She walked over to Mia and hugged her tight. "Thanks for everything, hun."

Mia squeezed her back and saw her off before she got back to work.

***

214

Mia realised that Westley seemed to have a lot of free time on his hands when he showed up at her office for the third time that week.

"Leah and Max may suspect something is going on," Mia said right before moaning as Wes rubbed her clit.

"Why would they think that?" he asked, hiking her skirt higher and groaning when he noticed she'd foregone underwear that day. "They're being so ridiculous."

"That's what I said," Mia replied, letting him lift her against the wall and wrapping her legs around him.

"We really should try telling them something convincing to have them all think we aren't doing anything," he said with a grin against her neck as he thrust into her.

"Um, yeah," Mia gasped, grasping futilely at the wall. "*Fuck.*"

"Definitely not that," he said and he bit her neck. She groaned.

"Maybe something a little more eloquent," he said, grabbing her ass tightly and licking where he'd bitten her. "With more words."

"Fuck you."

"No, fuck *you*," he chuckled, thrusting deeper with each word.

Minutes later they were both lying on her office couch, sated and boneless.

"You're going to get me fired, sexing up all the good air," Mia complained.

He laughed and the vibrations made Mia smile as she shifted with the movement. "You don't leave the office and won't need to take breaks if I keep you here. I'm saving them money."

"Not if I'm not efficient," she said drily. "What do you tell your colleagues? That you're off for a bit of debauchery?"

"That sounds so proper," he chuckled. "I tell them I'm out for a *merger.*"

"Classy," she snorted.

She sighed, deciding it was time to get back to the real world and earn her pay check. "I have to kick you out now."

He sighed as she put her clothes back on the right way. "I know. See you tonight?"

Mia smiled slowly, languid in the afterglow before her brain helped remind her of her schedule.

"Oh no," she groaned. "Can't tonight. It's girls' night at Leah's."

"Poor Lehman," Westley said. "Wait, screw him. Poor *me*."

"Truly tragic, yes," she teased.

"I'll see you when you get home then," he said and kissed her cheek. "We can play catch-up."

Mia blinked and then smiled, liking the sound of that 'Home'.

Hours later, she was at her friend's house, pigging out on ice-cream and cookie dough and writing down supportive reviews for pornos.

"You did your very best, Miss Jessica Cummingston. When you took that money shot, you left tears not only in your eyes, but mine as well."

Leah gave her a thumbs up and turned her screen to show Mia hers. "I can't review this. He asked 'who's your daddy?' and she burst into tears saying she didn't know."

"It ended there?"

"He stopped and hugged her. I'm too emotional to review it."

"Why is all your porn sad?"

"I guess my marriage is too happy. Oh!" she said suddenly. "Someone needs a good idea for a child's birthday party!" She started typing furiously.

Mia laughed. "I'm done with my good deeds for today. Let's watch a movie."

"The Notebook?"

"Kill me."

"The Notebook it is."

Leah finished giving detailed advice to the MotherOfThree69 and closed her laptop. She'd already chosen the movie earlier.

"Why do you make me watch this?" Mia asked.

"Because you never finish it."

"Why can't we start from somewhere near the middle?"

"Because you barely make it through the middle. I need you to experience the whole thing. It's my favourite movie."

"Can't we watch a horror? Or a super hero movie? Or porn?"

"We just watched porn."

"That was for motivational purposes."

Leah won in the end and her friend was out like a light by the time half the movie was gone.

Mia glared at Leah and was tempted to change the movie but Leah would just make her try to watch it again.

Her phone buzzed by her side. She looked at her screen and smiled.

It was a message from Westley.

She read it a few times before it registered.

W: *I'm here. Come outside.*

Mia stared at her phone. "What?"

J: *Wrong number?*

W: *Get your ass out here now.*

Mia looked over at Leah and was about to tell Westley to scram when he sent a picture of Leah's house. And then one of him looking sad.

She chuckled quietly and then edged off of the bed.

She'd just go see what he wanted.

She'd only be a few minutes. Leah would never know she was gone.

Mia snuck out of the house quietly.

She smiled when she spotted Westley's car parked around the corner.

He was leaning against it, losing extremely pleased with himself for having gotten her to come out at all. His blue eyes shone with victory. And desire.

"What are you-"

He pulled her to him and kissed her senseless.

Mia was shivering and out of breath by the time he stopped kissing her.

"Hello," he said with a wicked smile.

Mia's face grew warm and she almost smacked him.

He opened the door to the backseat and she climbed in.

Once he sat next to her, his mouth barely left hers, only pulling away to tell her how beautiful, how hot, how *wet* she was...

Mia moaned as he grabbed her, feeling every inch of him heat up with desire for her. It was maddening.

Her pyjama bottoms were tossed aside and she groaned when he grabbed the sides of her thighs and entered her slowly.

Mia grabbed onto his hair, kissing him deeply.

His hands roamed her body as she started to ride him, touching everywhere he'd already explored like it was new all over again.

Westley let out a guttural groan when Mia *squeezed*, thrusting faster, panting and throbbing as her pelvis beat continuously against his thighs.

It lasted forever but was over too soon.

They lay panting, holding onto each other and occasionally letting out giggles and chuckles at the ridiculousness of it all.

Westley helped her get dressed and tucked himself back in.

"So... how was your day?" he asked pleasantly.

Mia laughed. "Really? Small talk now?"

He nodded. "I wanna know how your day went, without me in it."

"So narcissistic," she observed.

He kissed her softly. "Mine was boring without you."

Mia smiled against his mouth as he kissed her. "I need to go, Wes," she whispered. "Leah..."

"I know," he sighed. He helped her out of the car and the two of them stood staring at each other for a moment in the bright moonlight.

Mia gestured toward her clothes. "How's everything?"

Westley looked her over. "Perfect," he said, eyes warm. "Not a hair out of place that wasn't already. Leah won't notice a thing."

"Hello Wes."

Wes started and Mia let out a small sound of surprise. They both turned to find Leah standing a few feet away, arms crossed.

Westley beamed, putting on the charm. "Leah, good to see you. I was just about to come in a say hello. I uh... was in the neighbourhood-"

"-of Mia' vagina?" she finished.

Mia's face grew warm and she groaned. "Kill me now."

"Sounded like he already did."

"Voyeur," Westley said, changing tactics.

"Be quieter next time," she said, rolling her eyes.

"I'm… gonna go now," Westley said, edging back toward the car.

Leah waved. "Bye, Wes."

Westley waved at her and looked at Mia.

"Don't leave me," Mia whispered harshly.

"You're a strong independent woman who don't need no man," he whispered back and got into the car.

"Bastard," she muttered and heard Leah agree.

Mia turned with a bright smile. "So, let's hit the sack and-"

"Explain."

Mia sighed. "It's just fun."

"Really? You both agreed to a *fun* arrangement?"

It occurred to her that they hadn't really talked about it and that was pretty much her assuming but she was pretty sure they were on the same page so she said, "Yeah. Means nothing."

Leah sighed. "So is this why you stopped fighting?"

Mia did her best to look scandalized. "What? Of course not. We still fight. We just don't want you losing any more money."

"How considerate."

Mia nodded. "Can we go back in now?"

"This can't end well, Mia," Leah said instead of answering that but she turned and they started walking back to the house. "One of you will get hurt."

Mia knew this was exactly what Leah would say and figured it was why she hadn't mentioned the shift in her relationship with Westley to her friend.

"I don't mean to scold you," Leah said, sounding apologetic. "But just ask yourself this... If it's all fun and games, how would you feel if he started seeing someone?"

The question made a sharp pain in her chest but Mia shrugged, not willing to deal with it there in the middle of the night on the street outside. There'd been fooling around a little over a week. That didn't mean she wanted to *date* him for real... did it?

"I wouldn't care," she answered, hoping Leah wouldn't be able to tell that she wasn't quite sure.

"Lie to me if you must," Leah said. "But not to yourself. You're both adults and you've been living together for some months now. It wouldn't be the worst thing if you actually started to like each other and wanted a relationship. You know I don't believe in 'friends with benefits'."

"Only because Lehmann refused it and married you instead," Mia said and Leah pinched her, laughing.

"I was young and foolish then."

"It happened two years ago."

"Yes, yes. Well now, since you're all sexed up and have no excuses, we are going to watch The Notebook again and if you fall asleep this time, I will murder you."

Mia groaned. "Fine"

She knew Leah had let their conversation go so they wouldn't get into a fight but she didn't want to think about it.

It was just fun.

No matter what her heart told her.

"Enough of this," Leah said, wrapping an arm around Mia. "No more talk of men if we aren't insulting or slobbering over them. That's what girls' night is about after all."

Mia chuckled, feeling lighter as her friend led her back in.

***

Mia spent the weekend with Leah and texting Westley back every moment she was free. He didn't show up again only because Leah threatened him saying Mia was hers for the weekend.

When Mia got back home, Westley was at the door waiting. He kissed her within an inch of her life and when she thought it would lead to something more, he just took a bath with her and then put a movie on for them to watch.

It was... nice.

They spent their evenings talking, making out and just being in each other's company. They didn't even always end up having sex and Mia wondered if they were breaking their own rules.

It was almost like they were dating.

The night she gave him a long massage after he'd had a long day at work, she realised maybe, just maybe there was a lot more to it than she thought.

She'd laid in his bed, with him holding her close, listening to him sleep and when she'd tried to get up to go to her own bed, he'd held her tighter and asked her to stay with him.

She'd kissed him softly and settled back down.

When Mia woke up to another weekend with the familiar scent of bacon and eggs that preceded an amazing full English breakfast. she stretched and smiled, feeling blissful and content.

It was scary as hell.

It wasn't that she hated it, just that she was suspicious. And having dated the train wreck that was Eric, she didn't want to be falling for someone who was halfway out the door.

Her phone vibrated on Westley's table and she picked it up.

'We need to talk. Please, it's urgent'.

It was a message from Eric and she snorted.

He'd started texting a lot more often. He'd apparently realised Emily wasn't the right one for him. He was saying all the usual things- he missed her, he just wanted to talk, he just wanted to say hello...

He'd added a few of the ones he used when he was worried that she was ignoring him. *I need your help, I can't turn to anyone else, my grandmother had a heart attack last night...*

She'd lost count of the number of times over the years that Eric's grandmother had suffered some sort of health issue around the time he seemed to be trying to talk to her.

She marvelled at how easy it had always been for him to get her to come running.

She shook her head and blocked the new number he was using to try reach her.

She heard Westley call her name softly and looked up at the door.

He was shirtless and only had a pair of sweats on. Mia eyed him appreciatively but her stomach growled.

"Breakfast," he announced with a knowing smile.

She nodded and got out of bed, telling him to give her a minute.

In the bathroom, she took in a deep breath.

She would see if he felt the same way about her.

She'd just do it.

How hard could it be to just broach the subject?

The kitchen island was set beautifully and Wes had even added roses in a vase on the raised counter. Mia smiled when she saw it and sat down opposite him in her usual seat.

She cleared her throat. "So... Leah seems to think we're getting attached."

Her plan for nonchalance must have failed because he gave her an odd look and kissed her cheek before plating her sunny side up eggs. "Are we?"

She played with her hair, watching him. "I don't know. Does the thought of me with another man bother you?"

He sat across from her and raised an eyebrow at her., "Does the thought of me with another woman bother *you*?"

She hesitated and let out a small, "No."

"So should we go on some dates? Prove to Leah we aren't...*attached*?" he teased.

She shrugged, thinking that wasn't at all how she'd wanted it to go. "If that's what you want to do...:"

He nodded and sipped some juice. "Okay, I'll need to find some unsuspecting woman and unleash my charm and-"

"Gosh, you're not a serial killer," she said shortly. "Just ask out the first attractive woman you see. She'll probably say yes."

He seemed to mull that over and she felt her chest clench. "Okay," he said finally. "Mia will you go out with me?"

She had just put a mouthful of baked beans into her mouth and the question registered slowly. She gaped and some fell out.

"Huh," he said plainly. "That's a first."

She felt her face heat up, taking the napkin he offered and cleaning the table while she swallowed. "What?"

"I don't know if you're still in denial but I don't want to see other people," he said, seemingly bored with the conversation. As if it was obvious. "Loathe as I am to admit it, Leah was right."

Mia' eyes narrowed. "She was right? About what? What are you saying?"

"I'm saying I want you. I want to date you. Properly," he said, being as clear as he could be.

"You can't mean that. Dating me would be... weird." She paused and then said, "I like romance."

"I can be very romantic," he replied taking a rose from the vase and putting its stem in his mouth.

"You're so lucky those don't have thorns," she muttered.

He ignored that and wriggled his eyebrows at her.

Mia moved to get up and walk away. He clearly wasn't going to take this seriously. Westley quickly stood in front of her and picked her up.

He kept waggling his eyebrows the whole time and Mia thought she was going to lose it. In anger or laughter, she didn't know.

He held her close and carried her back to his bedroom.

He threw her onto the bed and she yelled out in surprise.

Westley took the rose from his mouth, ripped the petals off and sprinkled them over her body. She stared blankly.

"*Romance,*" he whispered huskily.

Mia stopped holding her laughter in then and Westley smiled, joining her on the bed and waiting her laughter out.

"Will you give us a chance?" he asked when even her giggles had subsided.

"That was rubbish...," she kissed him softly. "But yes."

"Yes?" he asked unsurely and she nodded.

"Let's try it out. If it doesn't work out, we won't see each other again after our last month here is over. If it does… "

Westley frowned. "What are your misgivings exactly?"

"That you're not sure about this," she said truthfully.

Westley sighed and grabbed his phone. He put a finger to her lips and dialled Leah's number, putting her on loudspeaker. He spoke immediately she picked up.

"Leah, you know I love Mia right?"

"Oh wow, did you just figure it out?" she laughed.

"I thought it was obvious," he muttered, looking Mia in the eye. "But does Mia know?"

"Oh Honey," Leah snorted. "If you didn't tell her the exact words slowly while giving her an in-depth visual presentation of your feelings, she knows nothing."

"Thanks."

"No problem."

He hung up and stared at Mia pointedly.

"Let's be logical about this."

"I feel like you both just insulted my intelligence-"

"We did but let's look at the facts."

"Facts?" she asked, struggling to keep the amused confusion out of her voice.

"I love you, you love me, Eric is a wanker and Gertrude is a terrible name for a wife."

Mia waited a few seconds before she laughed. "What? Wes-"

"I won't change my mind. And I don't need to think about it," he cut her off. "I want to do this with you. It's as simple as that."

"Do what?"

He got down on one knee and Mia raised an eyebrow at him. "Mia Rhodes, will you move in with me?"

Mia laughed, nodding. "Okay."

Max would probably owe Leah a lot of money.

-

Epilogue: Cookbook

Six months later

-

Mia couldn't see past the bags in front of her and she groaned.

"Wes! Move!"

Westley, struggling with his own grocery bags, groaned back at her.

"Your boyfriend left presents again."

Mia cursed and peeked around the brown paper bags.

Their front door was blocked by dozens of roses.

"Do you think he believes I'm allergic and this is his attempt to kill me?" Wes asked as he finally got the door open and stepped over the bags.

Mia followed his lead, carefully going into their home.

"Shall we call the cops?" he asked.

Mia chuckled. "Again?"

Once her relationship with Westley had gone public, Eric had gone from just texting her to going the whole nine yards. He'd been trying to woo her and win her back and sent flowers every Wednesday, to their home, to her office and even to her parents' house. He said he was a fool to have ever let her go and just wanted them to work things out.

When he'd realised she'd blocked his number, he'd somehow gotten Westley's number and begged the man to let him speak to Mia.

Westley had told him he would hand over the phone as soon as they were done having sex.

"This isn't normal," Wes said, tiredly. "He's obsessed. I mean, you're hot but-"

She gave him a look daring him to finish his sentence. He kissed her. "You're *mine*. Also, if he ever comes near you, I'll kill him."

At Mia's raised eyebrow, he added, "Accidentally, of course."

"Of course."

They heard a loud squeal outside. "OH MY GOSH, DID THEY *FINALLY* DIE?"

Mia sighed as Max walked in, stomping on the flowers, too lazy to lift his feet. He saw them standing at their counter and said, "Oh, you're both fine."

Leah chuckled behind him. "We weren't completely sure that the flowers weren't here as some sort of memorial site."

Lehman came in after his wife, picking through the flowers and tucking a purple rose into his shirt pocket.

"Don't worry," Max said, opening their fridge and judging their beer. "We didn't place any bets. Just out of curiosity, though, am I in your will?"

Mia blinked at him. "I have a will?"

"Are you even an adult?" Max asked with a disappointed snort.

"I come bearing gifts!" Leah said, pulling out a paper. "George helped us get it done right away."

Mia looked at the paper and hugged Leah.

The restraining order was clear and George had added extra protection for them around their house and their neighbours and from the extra paper that looked like a neighbourhood bulletin, just hours before, Eric had been arrested driving to their house with large boxes of chocolates.

"I never thought I'd see the day Eric was begging to have you back," Leah said. "It feels good. Creepy, but good."

"Let's hurry this up," Max said, sipping his beer. "I got my sister's boyfriend's cousin's Netflix password and microwave popcorn. I'm ready to bond with you guys."

"Why not just pay for your own subscription?" Lehman asked, thanking Leah when she handed him a beer.

"It's not the same."

Minutes later, they were all in the lounge, arguing over what to watch.

Mia sided with Westley's choice and he kissed her cheek to the disgust of Max who told them they were grossing him out and cheating by siding with each other.

Mia flipped him off, the ring on her finger catching the light and drawing an exaggerated eye roll from Max.

Lehman voted against The Notebook and Leah gaped at him. He shrugged in apology and she promised justice would be served when they got home.

"Now that you've all voted," Max announced, "I want you to know I don't give a damn cause we're watching what I want."

He proceeded to ignore their protests and go about introducing their movie for the evening.

Wes held Mia close and she settled comfortably into him.

"I hate you," she whispered to him.

He smiled and kissed her in answer.

-

The End

CPSIA information can be obtained
at www.ICGtesting.com
Printed in the USA
LVHW092334011019
632916LV00001B/303/P